"I, milord, am not one of your possessions!"

Margaret Chilton looked directly at the tall figure as he raised his brows and began circling slowly around her.

"Edward had his reasons."

Margaret said nothing. She stared ahead in dead silence. A sudden gust of wind took the cloak's hood from her hair and blew the cloud of softness about her wistful blue eyes.

"Your father insisted on settling his daughter in a prominent family? Is that why you were marrying Corleal?" Lord Ballender watched her carefully while he questioned her. "You were obedient to your parents, weren't you, hm? Englishwomen are like that. No will of their own."

Margaret turned abruptly in an attempt to dart away. But he caught her and spun her about in time to see tears of hot anger making deep pools of her eyes.

Lord Ballender held her firmly and looked into the defiance burning on her face. "My arrows hit too close, did they?" His laugh rang out in the silence of their isolation. The corner of his mouth curved up to reveal a perfect set of white teeth in that ruggedly handsome face. "So now I should ask your pardon, eh? I ask pardon of no one and will not begin now."

Captive's Promise

JEANNE CHEYNEY

BOOKS
of the Zondervan Publishing House
Grand Rapids, Michigan

A Note from the Author:

I love to hear from my readers! You may correspond with me by writing:
    Jeanne Cheyney
    Author Relations
    1415 Lake Drive, S.E.
    Grand Rapids, MI 49506

CAPTIVE'S PROMISE
Copyright © 1988 by Jeanne Cheyney

Serenade/Saga is an imprint of Zondervan Publishing House,
1415 Lake Drive, S.E., Grand Rapids, MI 49506.

ISBN 0-310-47561-9

Scripture quotations are taken from the Geneva Bible.

Edited by Nancye Willis
Designed by Kim Koning

Printed in the United States of America

88 89 90 91 92 / DP / 8 7 6 5 4 3 2 1

To John Knox,
whose ancient letters
provided me with
the "eyes" to look
into the past

chapter
1

England, 1558

MARGARET CHILTON turned her great, blue eyes in an anxious glance toward the mass of gathering clouds as she, her father, and their servants left the ship at Sandsfield quay.

And later, she turned those same bewildered eyes to the unfamiliar scenery that greeted her—the ancient Corleal road, along which, single-file, they began to ride. She sat sidesaddle on her mount, straight and resolute as an arrow, but with little comprehension of the facts of this journey. She knew only that somewhere in this desolate countryside awaited the man destined to become her husband—in exactly three days.

"How much farther are we to travel, Father?" With concern cutting across her words, Margaret aimed her question solely at Lord Chilton, sitting astride his white stallion ahead of her.

"A fair distance." He didn't turn his head to toss her the terse response. His answer totally lacked his usual warmth and affection for his only daughter, and his eyes kept a steadfast vigil on the rutted, muddy road before them. Margaret noted his visible anger, which she knew to be caused by the ill winds that had blown their ship off course, causing their late arrival.

Noting the uneasiness in his words, Margaret searched the landscape before her. In the whole of the scene, not one trace of a tree was visible anywhere in the barren northern landscape bordering Scotland. She refused to admit that the thought of being owned by Lord Corleal, and living in this harsh land—dangerously close to the wild, lawless Scots rebels—left her numb and unfeeling. But a promise was a promise. She'd not go back on her sacred word. Ever.

"Lord," she whispered fearfully under her breath, raising her eyes heavenward as she sent up her appeal, "please go with us."

Lord Chilton, riding alongside his armed servants at the head of the procession, also lifted his face to the skies, but for a different reason. The rain that had threatened earlier began to fall in earnest, making the miserable marsh road and somber hills more bleak and lonely in the gloomy mists of darkness.

The party began snaking its way south at the ancient village of Bryth, whose fortified church was nestled between peel towers. Margaret knew her father would refuse to stop at an inn, for he deplored the very idea of spending a night in a bug-infested bed, and would choose instead to brave the fearful oncoming darkness. He urged the horses to a faster pace over the rough wet road clinging to the slight valley between low treeless bluffs and rain-drenched gorse.

After half an hour, the drizzle ceased. A faint touch of setting sun seeped through the parting clouds long enough to cast a glorious amber wash over the landscape. In silent awe, Margaret watched the gradual changing of color in the shifting skies melt into moonlit darkness.

Following one more hour of riding, the lead servant spotted action on the horizon, calling out to the family and servants behind him. "Movement ahead, milord!"

Margaret drew in her breath, realizing her fate was sealed—for the whole of her lifetime—in that patch of approaching motion. Her slim fingers moved without volition to clutch at the cloak's neckline. In the light of the full moon, she spotted what she assumed to be her betrothed's men, coming to meet the caravan.

She almost welcomed their arrival, for the penetrating chill and darkness of night made her forget her reluctance to reach Lord Corleal's castle—at least, there, she might bask in the warmth of a roaring fire. Margaret cast a hasty glance behind her, toward the servants' packhorses loaded with her wedding garments. An unspoken apprehension wrapped itself around each member of the party, as clammy as sodden, clinging silk.

The distant horsemen disappeared for a time while the procession pushed forward, following along the moon-bathed road and onto a rise near the river. Lord Chilton's lead servant steadied the lantern for a better view of the rutted road, while his master strained his eyes forward to determine what lay ahead and attempted to settle the nervous, skittish movements of his horse.

Margaret's faithful maid pulled her horse alongside. With the air of a protective mother, she mouthed hasty words of encouragement: "In just a few moments you will see your betrothed waiting for you, milady." Then in more somber tones she added, "Poor dear. You must be dreadfully weary. But one word from Lord Corleal will revive you and drive thoughts of this miserable journey from your mind."

Margaret returned a touch of a smile. "I'm no more weary than the rest," she assured the woman. She shifted her position and looked ahead, welcoming the thought of friendly servants meeting them on their journey. But as the Chilton retinue pressed over the final moonlit summit, a flurry of armed horsemen descended upon them with a suddenness that startled the caravan's horses into a frenzy of wild lunging. These were not Lord Corleal's men, but a marauding band of highwaymen, bent on relieving them of their belongings!

The first Chilton horse reared with savage fury, dumping the lead servant from his saddle with a force that sent him sailing headlong into the river. The remaining beasts pitched forward, down the sudden descent of the low bluffs into the stream.

Lord Chilton and Margaret were flung like sparks from blazing logs, and Margaret's ears recorded a sickening thump as her father's head struck a rock in the river. His partially submerged body lay motionless beneath the weight of his shaking stallion, its leg broken and helpless. Margaret herself was catapulted onto a bed of spiny broom, the pointed ends jabbing her face.

Her head spun and her vision blurred. In every direction the frenzied servants fled, with captors in fevered pursuit. Spears flashed in the moonlight.

When she shook her head and opened her eyes, Margaret witnessed in a daze the grisly scene before her. In a matter of seconds, horsemen gathered round, snatching rich garments from the body of her father and from the packhorses. Filthy fingers tore at pristine folds of silks and satins—her family's possessions!

The savages triumphed with glee, holding up their booty in the moonlight. When her dulled senses rallied sufficiently, she was filled with an overwhelming fury and revulsion. How dare the brutes lay hands on her father and their valuable stores! She groped for leverage to rise, unaware that her headdress lay a distance beyond, amidst the gorse. Margaret's long hair tumbled over her shoulder in disarray without the restricting headcovering.

She screamed with all the strength left in her body. "Get them to shore! They'll drown!" She lurched forward, her legs tangled in her voluminous garments. The men grabbed her and stood her on her feet.

"What have we here?" one shouted. "A young wildcat! Aha! I like that!"

Margaret was overcome with fright. Frantically, she clawed at them until a pair of firm, powerful hands grasped her body, forcing restraint.

"Never touched a *lady* before, I didna'," laughed one of the men.

She tore loose from his grasp and ran toward the river's edge as another man grabbed her roughly, subduing her with brute force.

"He's dead. Can't you see that?" The man snarled. A finality in his tone made Margaret's stunned face turn white from shock.

Trembling and staring at her father lying in the water she whispered, "No. No, it's not true. You're lying. You're lying!" But even as her voice rose in pitch, she detected no movement. Reason told her that the man's words were true. Hatred and terror overwhelmed her as she viewed the wild, towering men glaring down at her.

"Kill 'er and let's be gone!" urged the older man, who was dangling her father's cloak from his fingers. "Kill 'er like the rest, I say."

"No." A young man stepped forward. "No killing. Lord Ballender's orders. We got our cattle back, the Arabian and the packhorses. That's enough."

"You're a fool, Edward." The anger in the man's voice cut as a knife to challenge.

The man called Edward silently pulled Margaret from the men's grasp. As he did so, Margaret sank to the ground, weeping uncontrollably. He stood with legs apart, hands on hips, looking down at her.

"Go on! Hurry!" He motioned impatiently to the others. "I'll catch up!"

They obeyed, save one man who waited behind, holding onto the reins of Edward's horse, and those of the Arabian Margaret had been riding, and watching anxiously the departure of the others, packhorses in tow. Cattle nudged one another along at the insistence of the men's long pointed spears.

Margaret's face was hidden from view. She pressed her lips firmly together, closing her eyes and putting her hands to her mouth to quell fresh sobs rising from her throat. "Now get up," came the rough command.

Fearfully she opened her eyes. At that moment, Margaret spotted a dark patch at the edge of the gorse. She let her cloak sweep forward to hide the motion while her hand grasped her father's purse and drew it hastily into the folds of her riding garment. The swift movement went undetected by her captor.

"I am betrothed to the Lord of Corleal," she blurted out, in an attempt to appeal to whatever sense of fairness this brute might possess. A paralyzing fear clawed at her senses. Again her voice gave way and she choked back a sob. "We are to be married in three days.

Please take me to him," she begged. "He will reward you well for delivering me unharmed to the castle."

"Ha!" Edward gloated. "All the more reason to keep you with us. He'd put me in that miserable stinking dungeon of his before I could blink, and I have no intention of rotting in that hole." He stood watching her, a contemptuous smile twisting his lips up one side of his face as his hand grasped the reins of his horse. He jerked the animal closer.

"Come on," the other man urged impatiently from his mount. "Let us begone!" His eyes turned in the direction of their fleeing companions before winging an imploring silent plea toward Edward.

Margaret's riding outfit was heavy and awkward, and the ground beneath her feet, uneven. Her heart raced like a ship caught in the blast of a storm. She knew her only hope was to run. In the instant he released her to grasp the reins, and in a short spurt of strength born of fear and fury, she wrenched loose and raced blindly for the river, holding high her tangled skirts in one last valiant effort to escape. But her captor moved even more quickly, and she found herself with him, on his horse.

"You vixen," he snarled between his teeth. With one hand he jerked a rope from his saddle; with the other, he gripped her firmly. He bound her hands so tightly together that she feared all feeling would disappear from her fingers.

As they galloped off, Margaret turned for one fleeting moment to snatch a glimpse of her beloved father through her tears. She slumped down, beaten. Her throat choked back fresh sobs of grief. Margaret knew these men who held her captive were Scots—wild border reivers—about whom she'd heard many fearful tales. They had raided Lord Corleal's fields and were returning across the border with their spoils—and with her. Her future had been forever doomed in the tragic span of fifteen minutes.

chapter
2

THE HORSE ON WHICH she sat raced past a low hill as Margaret got her first fleeting glimpse of the moonlit castle in the distance to the east—Corleal Castle. The formidable fortress's black girth rose stark and forbidding into the night sky. Its majestic walls rested on the raised summit that bore its weight. Deeply crenelated battlements topped the curtain walls. Towers pointed heavenward, unyielding and defiant, piercing the spring sky with their stalwart thrust.

What will Lord Corleal say when I don't arrive? she wondered frantically. *O God, let him find me quickly!*

The man on whose horse she rode was named Edward. That much she remembered of the horrible nightmare just begun. She knew, also, that she'd never be able to entirely erase from her mind the sight of her father's body submerged in the river. Nor would she forget the wild glee of the barbarians stripping the cloak from his back or the treasures from the horses—magnificent wedding garments meant solely for her.

The unyielding leather rope dug into her wrists, causing Margaret to force the movement of her hands continuously in order to keep them from growing numb. She would have pleaded with the man to loose the knot, but she determined she'd not speak a word or beg one phrase from the wretched lot of these vile men.

Margaret found it necessary, despite her desires otherwise, to lean on this hateful creature, if for no other reason than to keep from tumbling off. Her fair hair spilled over her shoulders and face, but she continued to look back, straining to detect a movement or sound indicating the approach of Lord Corleal's men in hot pursuit of the fleeing band of reivers. Nothing! Nothing visible but a cavernous glooming darkness that melted into a distance black as pitch and silent as death.

Edward tugged on the reins of Margaret's Arabian horse to keep it close beside him as they raced forward. Soon the party of his cohorts could be seen, and he pushed his mount to regain their company.

After riding for some distance, the band urged the herd of hesitant cattle across a moon-bathed river, showering watery spray in all directions, making a tumult that rent the stillness of night as they forded across and clambered noisily to the grassy knoll on the opposite side. They headed northwest to continue along the valley between low treeless hills. How far into the dreaded blackness this wild band would take her, she had no idea.

Her body was stiff with fatigue and fear. Her arm throbbed from the fall. But the men showed no sign of stopping. Margaret ached to plunge into a state of unconsciousness and then wake to find that this horror was no more than a terrifying dream.

The cold dampness of night increased in intensity. With it came a strong wind that blew Margaret's hair into a flying film of pale mist, causing her captor to curse aloud when it blew into his eyes.

"Get that miserable stuff out of my face!" he snarled impatiently.

"How can I? My hands are bound!" she snapped angrily at the man without turning to look his way.

Edward reined in. "Sit right there and don't move," he warned her stiffly. Leaping to the ground, he jerked Margaret to the rear of the horse. Then just as quickly, he jumped up in front of her. "Give me your hands." His order was brittle with contempt.

Margaret could do nothing but obey. While he tore at the knot, she winced with pain until her hands were loose enough for her to put one arm in front of him and the other around his waist, as ordered, on the other side.

"Don't bind me, for I'll hold on," she objected angrily, withdrawing her hands.

He drew both of her hands together, ignoring her pleas until she was bound securely, then kicked the sides of his stallion. He moved forward to catch up with the rest of the party, urging Margaret's mount at the same pace alongside.

She was forced to lean tightly against him, though her stomach rebelled at the stench from both his body and the clothing of the dark, homely fellow. Surely he'd not bathed for days, perhaps weeks, and when she could stand it no longer, she turned her face slowly to his hard muscular arms. Studying the sleeves of his leather coat for a moment, Margaret held her breath against the smell, opened her mouth and bit him through the covering until he screamed aloud with pain.

He drew the horse to a sudden halt and cursed her savagely as he loosed her hands. He swept her immediately to the ground, but she eluded his grasp, and backing against his horse, she screamed, "You must pay me heed!"

"No! I'll not!" He shook her soundly with the pressure of both his hands savagely digging into her forearms.

Margaret lashed out at him with her fists, but he simply grabbed them and twisted sharply until she cried out from the unbearable pain.

"You mustn't bind me! Do you hear?" she seethed between clenched teeth. "It causes me pain, and I can't bear to lean against you! You stink!" Margaret looked unflinchingly into his face, in the light of the moon, without wavering.

"For what reason did you bite me?"

"How else can I get you to listen?" she reasoned through tears of anger and frustration. "Where could I escape? I have no idea where we are or where we're going, but I will hold on. I *don't* want to lean against you. And *won't!*" Her eyes shot sparks of flint and her mouth formed a terse line that defied any brutal action he might inflict on her in retaliation.

He sighed. "I should have let them kill you and be done with it. I'm a fool as Uthred said. A cursed fool."

15

"Go ahead!" she urged, sobbing afresh. "Go on. Spear me through! I'd rather be dead than go with the lot of you!"

"Corleal deserves you. Every inch of you. It would serve him right!" With an outstetched hand, Edward leaned wearily against the horse as he pushed the hair back from his forehead with the other. "Get up on your own mount," he seethed, "and if you jump, I'll whip you to a thread of your life!"

Only the steady clomping of the horses' hoofs and the slow, labored tramping of the cattle broke the silence of the bleak windswept hills and valleys as they headed for the Scottish border.

Margaret's eyes strained continuously back through the inky rises from which they had come. She constantly searched for a movement, a house, or a light as she blinked back the pools in order to see more clearly. Each fruitless scan netted only sinking frustration, nothing more. In spite of valiant efforts to do otherwise, she wearily slumped down in her saddle, but she refused to give up. She'd never give up hope of being rescued. *Never!*

While her body rebelled against the punishing, endless jostling, Margaret watched the men urge the beasts forward to a broad silver-rippled river and ford across to the far side. Here the party stopped and let out a blood-curdling whoop. "Scotland! Aha!" The men raised their metal helmets at arms' length in wild salutes as Margaret's last connection with England snapped in two.

She adamantly refused any aid whatsoever in dismounting, though her legs were stiff from riding and from the cold, and she deemed necessary a few moments of leaning against her horse before she could move easily enough to walk about.

Margaret ambled slowly to the water's edge and stared back over the black ripples of the river's sparkling current. She wondered if Lord Corleal would find the body of her father and the servants early in the morning, and if he would believe her dead, as well, sunken beneath the surface of the stream. Once again, she relived the horrible scenes while the night winds snatched at the fresh salty drops when they overflowed and trickled down her cheeks to land on her heavy riding garment.

While two of the men started a small fire, Edward walked silently to Margaret and offered her his leather bottle. In spite of her strong desire to refuse, she was too thirsty to abstain. After quenching her thirst, she involuntarily shifted her gaze back over the silver-drenched ripples below and in the direction from which they had come.

"So!" gloated one of the men standing next to the fire, the flames mirroring in his flashing black eyes. "We got the best of the Englishmen again. I would be happy to do it to the lot of the devils!"

"We all would," uttered Uthred, "but I'd rather get the better of the cursed Frenchmen taking over our country. The time may yet come when we'll be able to *welcome* even the vile Englishmen to help us."

"The Regent Queen Mary and her sniveling French bullies be hanged. Yes! But for now, aha! What pleasure that gave me!" With his sword swinging at his side from a waist strap, the man reached over and smacked the white Arabian—Margaret's Arabian—on its flank. Soon others gathered round, inspecting the sleek white horse from its nose to its tail, and uttering admiring comments.

Margaret blinked back tears of fury at the sight and the sound of the impact of such unworthy hands on her prized horse—a gift to her from her father. But she kept silent, fearing the band's reprisals if she didn't.

The men circled their horses around the cattle with the stream behind them. They took metal plates from their saddles, added a little water, and poured in some meal from their small cloth pouches. Again Edward offered Margaret some of his fare: warm oatcakes from the fire. But she turned her head away. Her stomach could tolerate nothing. He merely shrugged and shoved the remains of the pasty cakes into his mouth before moving back toward the voices of the men preparing to take their rest. Each threw a coarse blanket on the ground for a few hours' rest before moving on.

Edward pitched a torn, dirty cover at Margaret's feet. Though her flesh crawled at the thought of it next to her clothing, she was too weary to object. She took it, drew her cloak closely about her, and lay down on the hard ground to rest.

"Don't try to slip away," he warned under his breath, "or I'll secure you to my wrist."

Margaret refused to answer. The idea of escape, she knew, was futile. She had no idea where she was, except for the chance thought that perhaps the nearby river emptied into Solway Bay, where her father's ship lay at anchor. When she was rolled securely and had her arm tucked comfortably underneath her head, Margaret stared into the starlit darkness of night.

Her thoughts drifted to the cold, damp dungeons her father had often described in the past. In these northern parts, dungeons filled up with rank, putrid water at night and left in their wake, clammy, stinking cells unfit for human habitation.

Others, her father had told her once, were funnel-shaped, a narrow opening at the top leading down into small windowless rooms beneath the earth. When prisoners were finally released after long periods of time below ground, they were blinded for life. Margaret shuddered uncontrollably. Surely these savages wouldn't put her in one of those. Would they? Was she truly a prize to them? Would they hold her for ransom? *Lord, I'm your child,* she wept quietly. *Keep me and return me to my betrothed, for I'm frightened of these men!*

The ground was hard and her farthingale—the padding around her waist to fashionably billow her skirt—was uncomfortable. The blanket stank. Margaret thought of Chilton Manor, her beloved childhood home, with its profusion of ivy and the willows' long spears reflecting in the lake. Servants had been left behind to manage the estate in her father's absence. As soon as word reached her cousin that her father had perished, he would claim his rightful ownership of her father's title, house, and lands as the nearest male heir.

She would no longer be welcome in her beloved home. It would not be hers to leisurely roam the gardens or woods, for pleasure, or pick the rhododendron blooms from the bushes. Again she felt a great restriction in her throat. Perhaps Lord Corleal would no longer want her now that she'd been with these savages. If that proved to be true, perhaps her cousin would offer her a home. Margaret's whole life was trampled in the dust and altered beyond reason. Tormented thoughts continued to race through her head as she lay staring into the velvet night sky—thoughts of her home and her father and fears for the future. Her frustration and sorrow deepened with the passing moments. *O God,* she cried out in silent weeping, *help me!*

Then Margaret was suddenly aware of the light touch of a hand on her foot. She shrank back in terror, drawing her feet more closely to her body and putting as much distance between that contact and her body as she possibly could. But quickly it withdrew. Was there actually a touch of concern in Edward's contact or was it a prelude to more brutish feelings? Her flesh prickled with uncontrollable fear. Drawing her cloak even more tightly about her, she felt the soft wad of her father's purse hidden safely inside her bosom. This was her one and only remaining connection with her family, other than the Arabian that was tethered with the savages' own horses.

Sometime during the hour, Margaret drifted into the sleep that follows complete exhaustion.

Long before faint streaks of dawn crept into the sky to burst the blackness of night apart, the men began to stir and roll their blankets in preparation for the last part of their journey. With the sounds of swords slapping against their leather breeches and boots, the party tossed bundles over their horses' backs and arranged their long spears before mounting.

Margaret rose with a stiffness in her joints and an agony of fear in her heart for what lay ahead. When her cover was folded, she faced the south once more and wondered if she could swim or follow the stream back to its source and escape to Corleal. The lure of the lapping current racing over the rocks drew her to its edge, but a firm hand forced her to a halt.

"Get up on the horse," said Edward. A few hours' sleep had apparently put a softer edge to his voice.

When she refused to turn, his touch of compassion turned to sudden fury as he dug his fingers into the heavy fabric about the flesh of her arm, causing her to wince from pain. "Let go of me," she hissed angrily.

"Then do as you're bid!" He tossed her onto her sleek white horse and took the reins securely, urging both animals forward as the party slowly wound its way in a northwesterly direction once again.

Margaret's body ached unbearably with each jostling of the animal's movements. She wondered how long she'd have to endure the agony of the wretched journey and how far into Scotland they would travel before reaching their destination.

At last her fear and curiosity took precedence over silent speculation. "Where are you taking me?" she asked flatly.

Edward kept his eyes ahead. "To our village."

"And what will you do with me when we get there?" she probed further. The thought of having to stay in the same house as one of these vile creatures was more than she could possibly tolerate.

"That depends on what we *decide* to do with you."

"You could head me in the right direction and let me walk back to the castle." Her response was laced with overriding concern.

At this Edward laughed. "So we could." Then he laughed again. "But several of us need wives. It depends on how fast you learn to cook and become a dutiful wife. We live no pampered existence here."

"You beast," she whispered fearfully, the words coated with contempt. "You wouldn't dare. I am betrothed to Lord Corleal. He will come looking for me as soon as he finds I'm gone." Oh, surely her Heavenly Father would see to it that Lord Corleal would come for her.

"That's unlikely," he pointed out. "You're in Scotland now and beyond his reach. He'll search the gullies for your body, and when he doesn't find you, he'll assume you drowned or your body was carried away."

Margaret bit her lip to control her fury. Corleal would not give up the search so easily. He would reason it out. With many of his cattle gone and his cowherds tied he would know what happened to her. And when he did come, she'd be watching and waiting. She'd get away from these savage men, somehow, if it took the rest of her life to accomplish it!

Slowly the mists rose. The sky turned from gray to blue and the gulls began to fly low over the water in search of food. With the dawn, Margaret got her initial, clear look at her captors. They were a fierce-looking lot with unkempt hair and beards covering their necks down to leather collars. Edward was slightly taller with a narrow nose and thick dark brows over black eyes—eyes that turned occasionally to study his pretty captive with curious, greedy glances in the light of dawn.

Margaret was aware that the party continued moving northwest. In the distance, she saw the stony, heath-covered moors—hills— still partially shrouded with heavy mists. She kept her eyes turned away from the men's leering glances when they stopped periodically, between wet, marshy bogs, to let the cattle graze on the fresh spring grasses before urging them on in that same northwesterly direction.

Only God knew what awaited her when they reached their destination.

chapter
3

By LATE MORNING, the men urged the cattle and horses onto a long red sandstone bridge, its many arches spanning a broad, rapidly flowing river. The uneven clopping of hoofs echoed and re-echoed across its length. The procession moved forward toward the walled village of Ballender.

Uthred took the lead. The party followed the narrow dirt wynd—a path between rows of houses and shop fronts to the cobbled High Street. Each dismounted at the stone Mercat—Market Cross—at the center of the village. Each, except Margaret. She refused to budge from her horse until she knew exactly what fate awaited her there.

By now, women and children spilled out from stone dwellings clustered along both the High Street and the smaller wynds, adding to the bustling activity of the villagers already in the streets. The people of Ballender immediately drew away from shop stalls to move toward the returning party of reivers, whose booty became of prime interest—that and Margaret on her white horse. She turned her face away from the gaping lot, pulling the hood of her cloak more closely about her face in disgust as Uthred took command.

"We have cattle aplenty for Lord Ballender and us!" he announced with triumph.

"But what about these?" One of the men shouted as he hoisted Lord Chilton's rich cloak high in the air. "Aha! We fared well!"

A cheer swelled from the swarm of villagers as they inspected with overriding curiosity the rich fabrics the elated men displayed in their outstretched hands.

"Put all here at the Cross," directed Uthred. "Lord Ballender will decide as to their disbursement."

Margaret's fingers clasped involuntarily over her mouth to stop the knot of revulsion—the size of a turnip—in her throat. It threatened to choke her as she watched in horror—her family's belongings were being pawed over by the common rabble, who ran their filthy fingers over the fine fabrics that were meant for her body alone. She pictured her own prized Arabian. What would become of her? And her wedding garments. Would they be parceled out to the miserable lot?

"The vile swine," she hissed under her breath. "How dare they!"

"What about the lady?" asked Edward when Uthred moved close enough to hear his question.

Without even a pause of consideration, Uthred tossed back an answer. "You and Robin have no one now that your mother's gone. And you need a wife. Take her with you for now until I speak with our Lord Ballender."

Margaret's heart froze within her. Surely she hadn't heard the man correctly. She *couldn't* have!

No sooner had his words issued beyond his teeth than a clattering of hoofs was heard, racing along the cobblestones of High Street. A horseman approached and jerked his black steed to a sudden halt.

"Lord Ballender," uttered Uthred with respect. "We fared well as you can see, plus unexpected treasures!" His hand swept out in an encompassing arc toward the array of garments and the prized horse in their midst.

The young nobleman sat straight and tall on his magnificent sleek stallion. With an unfathomable sweep of flashing black eyes, he beheld the treasures herded at the tiered base of the stone Mercat Cross. He motioned his mount toward the Arabian horse, studying the animal's nervous movements, as well as her proud head and sleek flanks. Then Gavin Ballender's curious glance shifted to the cloaked figure sitting sidesaddle.

A silence encompassed the gathering as Margaret cast Lord Ballender one fleeting glance. She lowered her eyes, but not her chin, and clamped her teeth tightly together, refusing to acknowledge the man studying her. But that one fleeting inspection conveyed to her alert mind that this young nobleman—a man of perhaps twenty-eight—was not only wildly handsome, but he displayed a determined will not easy to reckon with.

A strong, muscular body beneath the gray doublet—a close-fitting jacket—gave concrete evidence of powerful, broad shoulders, over which a black mantle was casually flung. Fitted crimson hose accentuated his long sinewy legs. His thick, unruly hair was black as ebony, matching a carefully trimmed beard and mustache. His narrow nose tapered from piercing black eyes under thick raven brows, and terminated at a firm, unyielding mouth. In every sense of the word, he was the epitome of dashing knighthood.

But Margaret refused to be swayed nor would she admit to a quickening of her pulse. She was betrothed. No man would lure her from unswerving allegiance to the man who, nineteen years before—at her birth—was made her intended by agreement of both her father and the father of Lord Corleal.

Without looking, Margaret could sense one ebony brow lifting in contemplation before he opened his mouth to phrase his question.

"Who are you?" the man demanded.

Her chin lifted a fraction higher as her eyes stared straight ahead without wavering. If she were taken to a dungeon, she'd not go weeping. She'd go as a proud Englishwoman to whatever fate awaited her.

"Lady Margaret Chilton, milord." Her answer was starkly simple, purposely emotionless.

For a moment he studied the young woman sitting silent and unyielding on her mount. Then as suddenly as he had arrived, Lord Ballender urged his black stallion back to the spot beneath the stone Mercat Cross once more. His eyes carefully searched the band of raiders.

"Edward," he demanded, watching the young man immediately draw close in obedience, "why did you bring this woman here?"

"We stumbled onto her and her party heading for Corleal Castle as we were leaving with the cattle. She was the only one of her family left alive after her father lunged down the descent into the river and the servants scattered."

Lord Ballender's ensuing commands were issued in a muted voice aimed solely for Edward's ears. Edward responded with a silent nod of understanding. Margaret could only conjecture, with mounting fear, the meaning of that whispered conversation.

When Edward finally spoke, it was to answer only, "Yes, milord."

Lord Ballender then instructed Uthred, "Bring the Arabian and the garments to the castle." With that, he dug his heels into the flanks of his stallion, and raced, with mantle billowing behind, down the main street of Ballender toward the castle on the outskirts of the village.

Margaret drew in her breath. Even a dungeon would be preferable to this—this loose bartering over her, as if she were a mere herring or a piece of woolen cloth. The thought of living in the same house with Edward was not only revolting but terrifying. She had the sudden urge to dig her heels into her mount, but past experience warned her that running would accomplish no purpose other than bringing her more hurt. Edward's fingers digging her flesh or a slap across the face would be the outcome of such an attempt even before she reached the bridge.

But I'll not become his wife, she determined, facing the wall with a will forged in iron. The set of her mouth formed a firm line mirroring the staunch, immovable resolve within her.

Edward led Margaret's horse to the end of High Street. Before the young man could offer her help, Margaret dismounted, and when Edward turned toward her, his slight smile flooded her with fear. *The wretch!* She jerked her hand away and cast him a look of contempt that merely made him throw back his head and laugh aloud. His black eyes sparkled. The smile on his face showed a row of yellow teeth as he said, "I like your spirit, wench. I do at that. It'll be a pleasure watching it break until you're as tame as my horse."

She shifted her tear-blurred eyes toward the proud Arabian standing obediently at her side. She decided to attempt a plea for the fate of her last worldly possession.

"Please," Margaret begged, with deep emotion lacing her voice, "allow me to keep my horse. Surely it's mere common decency since you've robbed me of everything else that was dear to me."

"You heard Lord Ballender," Edward snapped with finality, yielding not a whit to the emotional request. "The Arabian is his. We have neither money nor feed for another horse."

Refusing to give in to fresh tears, Margaret reached up to stroke the Arabian's neck. She swallowed to keep the choking lump from swelling in her throat. In her grief, she could barely breathe. She leaned her head against the animal's warm side. With a sweep of despair washing over her, she patted the sleek flanks of the faithful horse that had carried her wherever she had wanted to go in her beloved England for the past thee years. It was as if the last of her family was being wrenched from her grasp and taken away forever. Only God knew why.

When Margaret at last lifted her face and turned about, she saw someone approaching from a small attached room at the front of a stone dwelling nearby.

The house—if indeed it should be worthy to bear the appellation—was worse than her father's stable. Through a thin layer of tears misting her eyes, she stared into the dark eyes of a sober man of thirty-five leaning heavily on a wooden crutch. In his hand was a piece of purple velvet and a tailor's needle. For a moment, Margaret detected a show of respect from Edward before he explained the situation.

"We have us a cook, brother Robin. No doubt she'll need teaching, but she seems bright enough to learn."

"What have you done?" Robin questioned solemnly, no smile creasing his serious expression.

"Done? We did nothing but save her from the fate of becoming Corleal's wife." With this, Edward's hands rested on the leather coat covering his hips as he reacted with a short, mocking laugh. "You couldn't really expect us to take the cattle from under Lord Corleal's nose with one hand and give her over to him with the other, could you? He would have had us in that castle dungeon of his with one nod of his unreasonable head."

Slowly the tailor came forward, calm gravity commanding respect. He spoke directly to Edward. "You could have left her there," he reasoned.

"Hardly. The others would have grabbed her before my back was turned. Would you rather have her with some of the others or with us, Robin?" Edward's jaw jutted forward in a challenging pose that demanded an equally challenging response to the conditions at hand.

Robin's gaze remained on his younger brother's face in a steady assessment of the situation and of the explanation offered him. His slight build was crowned with a thin face and thick auburn hair matching his brows and neatly trimmed beard. He studied Margaret with dark, serious eyes. *So these two are brothers!* Margaret marveled. Surely two brothers could be no more dissimilar. What one lacked in common decency, the other obviously possessed in abundance.

"Does Lord Ballender know of this?" Robin asked at last.

"Yes." Edward failed to enlighten the older man of the details of his recent conversation. "Come, Robin, it was the only way. Besides, you've said yourself we needed a woman around the house to do the work."

The older brother said nothing. He turned slowly and concentrated on the state of events as he leaned heavily on his crutch. Then his eyes raised to the silent Margaret, who stood, the wind catching tendrils of her blond hair. Shifting his glance to his brother he ordered quietly, "Make the necessary arrangements in the house." And turning, Robin walked back to the small tailor shop.

"Come along," Edward demanded, looking at Margaret. "You can start learning to work right off. We have no servants to wait on us or spoil us."

Margaret let her eyes make a careful survey of the stone house. It was one story high with a wooden door and heather thatch on both the roof of the house and the top of the tiny shop. She cast a final, parting glance at her beloved mare—she knew she might never see her again. Edward took a determined hold on her arm.

"Let me alone," she ground out in anger. "I can manage without your help."

"Then move, wench, move!" With this he impatiently scooped Margaret up, carried her the few steps to the house, kicked open the door, and plopped her down unceremoniously—like a sack of oats—onto a pile of dried heather in one corner of a small room.

Margaret had no tears left, and within moments, complete exhaustion encompassed her. She slipped into unconsciousness, escaping for a time her overwhelming flood of sorrows.

chapter
4

WHEN MARGARET AWOKE in the main room of the tailor's cottage, smoke was curling upward from a peat fire burning brightly in a stone fireplace. In the dimly lit room, she lay still and surveyed the darkened interior.

Overhead, oak beams spanned the ceilings. At one end of the central chamber, a small window allowed sparse light to enter, illuminating the few adornments—an oak chest and piles of dried heather used for beds. Near the fireplace were chairs, a table, and a crude shelf for bowls and cups. An iron pot, hanging by a hook over the fire, threw off great clouds of steam.

A figure rose to sprinkle something into the pot before reaching for a spoon to stir the bubbling contents. Robin! But he said nothing nor did he glance her way. In a few moments, he took two bowls from the shelf, filled them with oatmeal, and placed the dishes on the table.

"Won't you come and eat with me?" he invited, moving to speak to her from the doorway.

Margaret pushed her long golden hair back over her shoulders and removed her cloak, folding it neatly across the heather bed.

"Thank you," she answered softly. Then making her way to the place Robin had set for her, she pulled out the chair and sat down at the table. Silently Margaret bowed her head and thanked God for placing her where she at least felt safe and would receive a measure of kindness from someone like Robin.

"Do you feel anger against God for what has happened to you?" he questioned.

Margaret's blue eyes immediately darted to Robin. For a moment she thought about the question before answering.

"If I believed he had forgotten me, yes, I would," she answered softly. "But he knows where I am." Even as she spoke these words of faith, she suddenly felt an overwhelming calm spreading over her, a Presence that entered her heart and buoyed her up, sending a fresh wave of hope surging through her being. She knew she wasn't alone. God was with her.

"I hope," Robin responded with a deep sigh, "that God hasn't forgotten our poor Scotland."

Whatever can he mean? Before she could comment, he rose and poured a little ale into a cup, handing it to her.

"I've got some dresses for you," he said, breaking the short silence. "That one you have on will hardly do for our life here." At this, Margaret was tempted to lash out at him, to tell him in no uncertain terms that she wanted no part of Scotland nor anything in it. But she knew she couldn't take her vengeance out on Robin. She had to believe that somehow God had his hand in sending her here to this miserable country.

"I realize," Robin added perceptively, "that you don't want to be here. But the fact is, milady, you are here and there is little we can do about it until Lord Ballender decides what is to be done with you. So, until that time," he pointed out, "try to fit in, for your sake as well as for ours."

"What," she asked hesitantly, "will Lord Ballender do with me?"

"I can't say."

With pleading showing in her large eyes, Margaret looked into Robin's face. "I must get back to England," she stated urgently, "for I am promised to Lord Corleal. In two days we are to be married!"

Robin's look brushed across the distraught features of her face. "As I said, I can't answer that." Then, rising, he added, "I must take leave of you and return to my work." With the help of the crutch, he walked toward a wooden door leading into his small shop. Robin turned and called back over his shoulder, "The dresses were my mother's. They're on the chest over there."

Margaret watched him go to the stool in the tidy shop, maneuver awkwardly onto the seat by means of his crutch, then pick up a green doublet. He began making small, careful stitches in the beautiful fabric. She wondered who in this village could possibly afford such luxury. Hesitating for a few moments, Margaret let her eyes study the man before turning to examine the clothes he had left for her to wear.

What Robin had pointed out was true. And since Robin seemed to respect her, she knew she had to make the best of her unfortunate situation and be civil to him. Her glance continued to linger on the tailor. Somehow, she felt that in Robin she had a friend—her only friend in the whole of this desolate country.

Yet, if the opportunity arose for her to escape, she doubted she could survive the wilds of the Scottish country. It seemed her only chance for rescue was to remain here—where Lord Corleal would surely come searching. And with Robin to care for her, and God to watch out for her, she had nothing to fear.

She picked up the rest of her meal and walked outside the hovel, through the rear door, to eat it. The putrid odor of dung was more than her sensibilities could any longer tolerate.

The bright sun shone on the stone dwellings and hills. As far as she could see, the landscape was as bare as a cooked soup bone, with no hedge or bush or tree—except for the land surrounding the bleak castle perched on its rock foundation to the rear of the village. A few trees were allowed to stand at the base, but all else was abject nakedness.

Could any land be uglier? She leaned heavily against the rear of the dwelling and let her gaze wander from one unattractive edifice to another, all of the same stone and thatch, all detestable and stark in design.

About each dwelling filthy children played with stones or engaged in games of leapfrog. But they left their games when they spotted her, to stand about and regard her, with incredibly blank expressions on their thin faces.

Margaret slowly spooned the last of the oatmeal into her mouth. Only her eyes raised to glimpse the curious group until they dispersed and resumed their play in another part of the village. With bowl and spoon in hand, she walked back into the house, deposited them on the table and turned to examine the dresses Robin had left on the chest.

Both gowns were made of wool and were old and worn; only one was fairly clean. Margaret wondered how she could put the fabric against her flesh. She realized her own clothing would not suffice if she must live here for any length of time before being rescued, and reluctantly entered a small room to remove her cumbersome gown. She rolled her riding garments into a neat bundle and placed them at one end of the bed of heather for a pillow.

As she was adjusting her petticoats and holding the wool fabric in her hands before slipping it over her head, Edward burst into the room carrying a huge bundle of dried heather. With his mouth agape, he stared at her bare shoulders. Margaret felt the rush of deep crimson sweep over her face as she clasped the gown to her body in a desperate effort to hide her indecency.

"Please leave," she ordered sharply. But he continued to regard her partially unclothed body. Shifting his gaze, after what seemed to Margaret an eternity, he strode over and deposited his armload of bedding in a corner of the main room. Then turning, he calmly walked out.

Margaret drew in her breath in angry frustration as she struggled with the clothing. Her eyes clouded with tears. It took forced effort to make her teeth clamp tightly together in order to keep from tossing abusive shouts at the closed door. She wrestled with the gown, finally succeeding in getting it in place. The fit was infinitely better than expected. It was plain, coarse wool with strings lacing the bodice together in a crossed fashion in the front. The cloth was light on her body after wearing the bulky English riding gown and full petticoats. She tucked her father's purse into her bosom.

The small neck ruff was dirty, so Margaret refused to put it about her for a collar. She held the ruff in her hand and folded the other dress over her arm as she turned toward the larger room. Her eyes made a sweeping search of the two rooms.

Margaret felt the acute need for an activity to ease her worry and her heartache. She studied the few tools used for cooking—the cooking pot, churn, bowls and cups. Then she looked at the floor—filthy! At the far end of the large room, straw was littered with manure. In no manner could she maintain a semblance of sanity unless it be cleaned. Margaret searched in vain for a broom, but in a far corner of the main room, she found a triangular tool resembling a spade.

Taking it up, she started to scrape at the the grime collected about the floor in layers. Her stomach wrenched at the mess, but she determined to rid the house of the squalor and stench if it took her all afternoon.

As Margaret moved about the room, she spotted a niche in the wall near the fireplace. In it was a large package in a frayed covering. She reached up and removed the weighty bundle from its storage cubicle. In carrying it to the doorway for a better look, she discovered the wrapping consisted of wool. Its obvious purpose was to keep the dampness from damaging the precious contents. Inside the bundle was a Bible written in English.

Surely these peasants were not able to read. But what else would explain the presence of such a costly book in such a crude dwelling? Margaret's heart soared beyond her surroundings—God had provided his Word for her. In it she could find the strength to endure what was to come and the hope that he would care for her and deliver her from what threatened to be a dreary existence. She spent a few minutes turning the pages with care, then carefully returned the Bible to its niche by the fireplace and her attention to her unfinished work.

Shoving the debris out the front door, Margaret glanced momentarily at Edward grooming his horse along the street in front of the house. He paused to study her when she came outside.

"Mother's garments are becoming to you," he called to her without stopping his work for more than a second. "She was about your height but much less fleshy. You fill it out very well in places where she lacked." Here he smiled and took up his currying.

His bold, ribald comments hit their mark and Margaret's face flushed crimson. Deciding to ignore her crude captor, and without looking his way, she found a sharp stone, then took water from a bucket in the corner and scrubbed the pot, churn, bowls, and cups until they glistened.

By late afternoon, Margaret allowed Robin, in his calm, gentle way, to show her how to prepare the evening meal of greens and fish. When the men came in to eat, Edward's eyes spotted the churn in the sun, scrubbed to a look of newness.

He bellowed like a cow separated from the rest of the herd. "You've ruined it, woman. Now we're in for a heap of bad luck as sure as anything!" With this, he gave the churn an angry kick. "Don't you know cleaning a churn is sure to bring about adversity? And we need all the luck we can get to rid ourselves of the rotten French!"

"If I have to keep house, it will be clean!" Margaret fumed angrily. "And if you don't like it, you can send me back to England!"

chapter
5

AFTER ONE NIGHT OF SHARING the house with the cattle and sheep tethered at the far end of the main room, Margaret decided the stone hut where the grain was stored, but for its rats, would be preferable to the stench she had experienced the night before. Before breakfast, she stated her aversions to the animals in the house. "I can't tolerate it," she announced firmly.

"We like it that way. The clartier the cozier," Edward voiced his reply. "But if you've a mind to, you are welcome to clean it out."

Furious, Margaret stalked outside with her breakfast. She had spent the previous day cleaning, and now she couldn't detect any sign that she had spent a moment's time trying to make the hovel a bit more pleasant. One thing was certain: Edward and Robin would offer no help; it befell her lot to do what she wanted done, disgusting and loathsome as the task might be.

Her thoughts turned wistfully to her father and his untimely death. She compared her present circumstances with the cleanliness of the estate that had been her home for nineteen years. A rush of homesickness engulfed her and Scotland became less real, as if she were living her life in a nightmare.

The brothers went out of the house discussing some matter of concern, ignoring her completely. They stood in front of Robin's shop. A few men gathered with them. Their faces mirrored deep inner conflict, manifesting itself in a flaying of arms and accompanying words that, more often than not, reached the boiling point. Periodically, Margaret caught the words "French" and "Regent" and "idle bellies."

Margaret wearily returned her bowl to the table and tackled the fresh animal refuse with the same pointed tool she'd used the day before.

The heated discussion raged on, whatever the subject, and Margaret became aware that Robin was a sort of moderator. Why were they discussing the French so vehemently?

After her cleaning was done, she walked to the front of the house and stood for a moment in the open doorway. A soft breeze blew from the southwest, bringing warmer air, and on that same breeze were carried more words—the words "tithes" and "fees" and "burials"—emanating from Robin's small tailor shop. Their anger, and its effect on her well-being, seemed of no importance.

She scooped up her alternate woolen dress and called to Edward. He was preparing to mount his horse. From his manner of dress and the sword at his side she surmised he was a guard at the nearby Ballender Castle.

"Have you a place where the washing is done?" she added impatiently.

"Yes. Down there." He pointed in the direction of the river at the bottom of the hill, beyond the town walls.

"In the river?" A look of incredulity flashed across Margaret's face. Her mind immediately flashed back to Chilton Manor with its special small house and the specific servants assigned to the washing of the garments of the Chilton family.

"No better place," he answered shortly, adding, "plenty of water." He regarded her for a moment, then warned, "Don't try to leave, for I'll be watching you from the castle battlements. I'll be upon you in a breath if you make such a move."

Margaret purposely ignored Edward's remarks. "I don't suppose you have soap," she asked flatly, knowing the answer he would give.

He clicked a directive to his stallion before he shot off down the street. His reply sailed back to her eardrums. "No."

Margaret pivoted about and started toward the gate in the wall surrounding Ballender—and in the direction of water flowing rapidly at the foot of the hill. "I don't know what the Regent and her French lieges are doing to these wretches," she fumed, "but whatever it is, they deserve it."

At first the village wives stopped their washing and singing to watch her, but when Margaret passed on without so much as a glance in their direction, they continued their rhythmic songs as they stamped upon the clothes in wooden tubs. The vile and brazen words drifted clearly to Margaret's ears despite her resolve to remain disinterested—words that mockingly referred to the despicable French priests. The women sang with abandon, giggling at the ribald meanings and always ending with the same refrain: "Hay trix, tryme go trix, under the greenwood tree."

Margaret scrubbed even harder, attempting to cleanse the air as she cleansed the garments. But the vocal filth continued. *The whole village—the whole country—is disgusting!* She must get away! Somehow.

Suddenly the singing stopped, and in its place Margaret became aware of the tinkling of a bell and the creaking of a cart as it advanced toward the sandstone bridge, from the east of Ballender along the valley bordering the rushing watercourse. Margaret turned her head and studied the small weathered conveyance and the driver in his attempt to avoid the watery bogs in the low fields beyond the river. The horse followed the path over the bridge into the village and stopped at the Mercat. Children ran out and women drew around to examine whatever it was the man had in his cart. *A peddler!*

Margaret wrung out her dress and made her way up the wynd and back to the house. She spread the gown on a pile of stones to dry. From her vantage point, she watched the women fingering the peddler's cloth, pots, and cups. One by one, the villagers disappeared into their houses, returning with eggs, butter, and sacks of oats and barley in exchange for his wares.

When the man was apparently satisfied that he'd done as much bartering as he was able, he clicked his tongue and the horse moved obediently along the narrow wynd toward the bridge once more.

Running her fingers through her matted hair, Margaret ran after the cart and caught up with the peddler as he neared the second arch of the bridge.

"Peddler!" she called after him. "Do you have a comb and a little soap?"

The man pulled his horse to a stop and stared at Margaret, assessing her with interest a moment before answering. No one asked for anything as useless—or as costly—as soap. "I have combs, but just one small piece of soap."

Margaret added quickly, "I'll buy them—with coins." She turned a moment, reached into her bosom, counted out the coins and handed him the cost of her purchases.

"When I go to Glasgow I can get you more soap, but it will be awhile before I return—a fortnight, maybe." He licked his lips eagerly at the sight of coins; they were in wretchedly short supply these days.

"Do you travel to England with your wares?" The sudden thought occurred to her—he might be able to help her.

"No. I don't cross over the border."

Margaret's sudden, bright ray of hope flickered to ashes as quickly as the flame of her hopes had risen. "Thank you," she sighed. Then turning, she headed toward the house with her precious soap and comb in her hands.

She lost no time in heating water, bathing, and washing her hair. After emptying the water, she carried the large Bible behind the house to a wide flat stone and read while she dried her blonde tresses. She ran the comb through the knots until each strand was neat and shiny, reflecting the rays of the sun in its pale glory. To be clean and have tidy hair once more elevated her tottering spirits a notch or two above the depths of despair.

From where she sat, Margaret could see the villagers carrying water in wooden buckets hung from poles across their shoulders. Horse-drawn carts clattered along the cobbled High Street. Women took baskets of eggs and reluctant sheep toward the castle. Small groups of men stood about the Mercat embroiling themselves in animated discussions about the popular, current subject, the French and the House of Guise, family of the Regent Mary, whose daughter was Mary Stuart, Queen of Scots.

Margaret knew something of the history of the rulers of England and Scotland. Mary Stuart had been the real queen of Scotland since the age of one week. Margaret had heard it said that Mary's mother's cunning brothers, Claude, Duke of Guise, and Charles, Cardinal of Lorraine, were the real powers behind the throne.

Slowly Margaret's gaze shifted to the castle, standing as the village's protective sentinel on its earthwork motte. While she watched, Lord Ballender—riding his familiar black stallion—burst from the castle yard and approached along the main street. He urged his steed across the long sandstone bridge spanning the river, his hair ruffling wildly in the spring air. From the far side, he headed toward the distant heathered moors, dotted with spiny shrubs of whin.

Margaret's eyes studied the dashing figure and pensively recalled the handsome features of the young nobleman at the Mercat the day before. Then forcing restraint on her errant thoughts, she turned her face again to the castle. It was enclosed with high curtain walls and circular corner towers. The square towerhouse rose four stories into the cloudy sky, with ancient red stones weathered by the elements. The windows were small-paned. On the north side circular turrets projected upward from the top floor. Did the castle enclose a fearful dungeon, dank and dark, filled with putrid water at night? And did Lord Ballender intend to banish her to such a prison?

This should have been my wedding day, she considered dejectedly. If she were with Lord Corleal now, as Lady Corleal, she would be dressed in her wedding garments instead of this coarse woolen peasant's dress. She would be ensconced in a fine castle—as fine as Ballender, she was sure—instead of sitting on a stone in the middle of more filth than in the whole of England. *O God, what will become of me?*

Maybe it would have been better if she had been killed in the raid on her traveling party—like her father. Her father! It was her hope that he had been given a Christian burial near Corleal. Even though the sun shone warm, she felt a sudden chill as she relived the tragedy, now seeming dreamlike in reflection. She forced herself to stem her weeping—great silent tears—for what might have been. Tears would change nothing. Surely Lord Corleal would come for her. Surely he had some idea about the identity of her abductors.

Margaret sighed and clasped the great Bible to her breast as she walked toward the fields. She stopped to look out over the rigs— the farm strips running vertically down the gradual slopes—and their produce. Meager weed-choked crops of oats and barley sprouted from barren, thin soil.

The sun brought out the glistening gold of Margaret's hair. The wind whipped it about as a cloud with little wisps catching on her long, dark lashes. She turned with a troubled heart back to the flat stone, seating herself once more before opening the book to read. Margaret was unaware of Robin's presence until she heard his voice behind her.

"Do you read, milady?" A look of surprise cut across his words.

"Yes."

The tailor moved very near and studied her face. "Do you read well?" His voice belied his mounting interest.

"Yes." She absently chewed on her lower lip, glancing at Robin and thinking how kind he was. She could never dislike him in the way she did the others, for he possessed a vast store of compassion and a decency that all the others lacked.

For a moment he remained silent. Then he asked, "Will you teach me to read?"

"If you don't know how to read, how is it that you own a costly Bible?"

"It was a gift. You see, I have always wanted to learn to read and write so I could help our people. Our French Regent and her priests and advisors have no compassion for the poor. They grow rich while we starve. That must cease. To be a leader, I must read. My family had no means to school me and no one in the village had the knowledge."

Margaret nodded silently. This man was sharing his deepest dreams. The idea that he had chosen her, a total stranger, to hear them somehow touched her.

Robin leaned heavily on his crutch and looked longingly at the book she held in her hand. His expression almost spoke aloud—almost told Margaret that he believed its pages truly held the key for his future and that of Scotland.

"I don't know your name," he said apologetically.

"Margaret. Margaret Chilton."

"Margaret—a pretty name—could you teach me to decipher the marks on those pages?" Then hesitating a moment he added, "Won't you call me Robin?"

In his face was mirrored a deep eagerness to learn. Although Margaret had until now felt no compulsion to help any of these abominable Scots, Robin *had* been kind to her. That, coupled with his gentle plea, was enough. She knew she wanted to help him. "I've never taught anyone to read before," she began apologetically, shrugging her shoulders in a helpless gesture.

"I'll try my best to learn well."

His fierce determination seemed as a rock. "When do you want to begin?"

"Right now. If you don't mind, I will sit next to you."

Margaret moved over to make room on the flat stone for Robin. He seated himself awkwardly with the aid of his crutch and his one good leg before turning to her with high expectations written in his eyes.

"We have no parchment or quill," she objected.

"We have the whole of God's earth beneath our feet and stones aplenty." He reached quickly for a small jagged rock nearby and handed it to the young woman seated next to him. Robin looked directly at her, with an air of expectancy that bespoke his fervent belief in the immediacy of the miracle of understanding the printed word.

Where to begin? After a moment's hesitation, Margaret concluded that the alphabet was the most logical beginning. She bent and scratched some letters in the dirt at their feet.

For the rest of the afternoon, Robin soaked up the rudiments of reading like parched earth greedily gulping rain. Never had a pupil been more apt, more eager to learn. In the zeal of her teaching, Margaret forgot her own anguish.

That evening after the supper dishes were put away, Margaret went to Robin's small workroom in the front of the house and sat next to him on a stool. She noticed that his fingers were clean and that his whole body smelled freshly scrubbed. The woolen shirt on his back was spotless. But it was the practicing of letters and sounds from the open Bible that drew her attention, for he had obviously mastered what she had taught him earlier.

Looking up at Margaret, Robin said, "I was told once that all these pages had important messages from God." He hesitated a moment, then added softly, "I used to sit and just hold the Book, and as I held it, I asked God to provide the means for me to read it. Now he is doing just that." Robin cut a piece of thread and put it into the eye of his needle. "While I work, would you read to me, Margaret?"

"Yes. But instead of starting at the beginning of the Bible, I will turn to one message in the New Testament, a message that is very special." Margaret turned to the Gospel of John and began reading the words slowly and carefully, putting emphasis on one of the verses in particular.

"For God so loved the world that He hath given His only begotten Son, that whosoever believeth in Him, should not perish, but have everlasting life—"

With suddenly heightened interest, Robin looked up from his stitching and asked, "Would you please read that part again?"

She complied. "Again," he begged.

She read it once more. "Margaret," he said a little breathlessly, "what wonderful promises God has written there." Then placing his sewing on his lap, he considered a moment before adding, "If God says, 'whosoever,' then he means me."

"Yes, Robin."

"And it's really true, then, that if I believe in him—believe in him with all my heart—I will be ready for God's Kingdom?"

"Yes, it's true. God will move into your heart if you commit your whole life to him and believe that he will do exactly as he says. I know. He did it for me."

"Yes," Robin answered excitedly. "Yes! It's a true message of hope! I do believe!" Robin cried. His brown eyes glistened as if touched by a brilliant ray. "My dreams are finally becoming a reality, for I have now reached the first step in my searching. God has begun his work in me and he'll not stop now!"

Margaret sat quietly, not wanting to interrupt the beauty of the moment while Robin contemplated the goodness of the Lord in bringing him the joy and inner peace of his newfound faith.

"Such joy must be shared," Robin said at last. "It's the work that God has given me to do. I see that now. And I will be faithful in bringing this wonderful message of hope to our people of Scotland, for they have been trodden down and discouraged far too long."

Picking up his stitching once more, Robin warned quietly, "Dangerous times are coming, Margaret. Our people need to be united under God—have a common faith—to fight against the enemy. Hordes of French soldiers, with their families, are pouring into our country at Leith—the seaport of Edinburgh. And the Regent allows them to demand food from our people. Our crops are too meager to feed our own people, let alone provide for these strangers." For a few moments Robin grew silent.

When he again opened his mouth to speak he explained, "Our Regent is a temporary ruler until her daughter, the child of our former king, comes of age. Mary will be our rightful ruler one day, but at this point, she is being schooled in France—and prepared to marry the son of the French king. Their allegiance and love is for France, not Scotland. Unless we can quell this, our country will become a French province." Robin's chin lifted. "But God will not permit that," he stated with deep, unwavering conviction borne of faith.

Margaret heard his heart's cry for his pitiful country. She knew this same obsession grasped the hearts of all the people of Scotland—the consuming desire to be set free from France's unjust domination. How long, she wondered, would it take? And what price would Robin and his countrymen have to pay for their freedom?

chapter
6

By MID-JUNE the northeasterly winds were soft, bringing a general rise both in the temperatures and in the spirits of the people. Margaret heated water to wash her hair with the additional soap the peddler had brought from Glasgow. For the first time in weeks she felt her sinking spirits rise to the level of bare minimum tolerance for her situation and for the wretched humanity of the filthy village. If it weren't for Robin, she knew she couldn't keep her wits about her one more day.

"Thank you, Lord, for Robin," Margaret breathed softly.

She sat on the flat rock to fluff her hair and pull the comb slowly through her long thick locks until the strands dried and began to curl once more at the edges.

Again Margaret thought about Robin. How serious he was! And what an eager mind he possessed. Unlike his brother, who gave not a thought to anything but village women and the alehouses, Robin was like one who had suddenly awakened from a deep sleep of many years' duration. Those calm brown eyes of his had come to life, had begun to shine with a luster, with the reading of the Scripture promises. For the first time in weeks, Margaret felt a smile crease her lips upward in thanksgiving for God's workings in Robin's life.

He continued to show Margaret the greatest respect, not once attempting to touch her, though at times he let his eyes rest upon her when he thought she did not see. He must know of her betrothal to Lord Corleal and of her intent to return to the home of her promised husband. That fact, no doubt, honor-bound him to treat her with respect.

Margaret placed her chin in her cupped hands to study the barren eastern expanse, the distant hills and valleys beyond the river. Two riders came into her line of vision, approaching, then turning suddenly to vanish as the wind. Margaret had little doubt that Lord Ballender was one of the riders; the other a young woman. She could hear their faint laughter and muffled calls to each other as they tore the summer air apart with their wild racing and abandon. The wind clutched at their mantles, billowing them as sails behind them.

For a few moments, Margaret continued to regard the pair, feeling an unwelcome increase of pulse at the sight of the dashing young man, remembering his piercing dark eyes and handsome physique. And for the first time in her life, she experienced an uncomfortable feeling she recognized as a touch of jealousy. Just as quietly as it had appeared, she clamped her lips tight and looked away to wrench such thoughts from her heart. She dared not allow such feelings to take hold.

She forced her thoughts to return immediately to Lord Corleal. If only she were now his bride; as Lady Corleal she would be carefree, with a heart as light as . . . the hearts of those two riders. Again Margaret sighed and looked away to the southeast in the direction of Corleal Castle.

Early in the mornings, after Edward left for his duties at the castle, Robin and Margaret sat by the open door to read. And when they finished, she set about her household tasks while he, too, mounted his horse to ride off toward Ballender Castle. He offered no explanation of his destination, so she went about her duties and tried to ignore the ritual. His whereabouts were, after all, none of her concern.

When her work at the house was ended, and she finished purchasing needed supplies at the open stalls of Ballender, she read or wandered into the fields to escape the curious eyes of the villagers. Her strolls took her through the meadows, and she let her woolen peasant skirt trail through patches of creamy meadow sweet as she reached down occasionally to pick a few select blooms to carry in her slender fingers back to the hovel to place on Robin's workbench.

The following week, on Wednesday morning, Robin woke with stomach pains and fever. Margaret tried to make him as comfortable as possible, but could do him little good. At midmorning, still not improved, he asked wearily, "What kind of day is it?"

"Cloudy, but the sun shines occasionally."

"I have a favor to ask."

Margaret knelt beside him and looked into Robin's feverish face as he spoke in soft, labored sentences.

"After our reading lessons," Robin explained, "I go to the castle and teach Gavin what you teach me. Since I am ill, you must take my place. You must take the Bible with you. Beneath and to the rear of the fortress, you will find a few plum and pear trees. As you approach that area, follow it around until you come to the orchard . . ." Robin paused, for his breathing was difficult. ". . . where a stone seat is among the trees. We meet there on nice days. Wear your cloak so you don't get chilled in case it should rain."

"Are you well enough to leave alone?"

"You are not to worry about me," Robin assured her. "It is of more import that you keep the appointment. Promise me you'll go?" He placed a feverish hand on hers to wait for her answer.

"I promise," she said.

"Good. Now go to the castle."

The distance to the castle was farther than it appeared from the house. Who was this Gavin of whom Robin had spoken? Perhaps he was Lord Ballender's son. Until now, she had not considered that Lord Ballender might have a wife and family. Of course! The young woman she had seen riding with him—she must be his wife. Chiseled in stone might have been her sudden determination to put Lord Ballender now and forever out of her mind. Such thoughts of a man were wrong. *Very wrong.*

Margaret looked to the trees behind the castle. As she walked toward the fortress, carrying the heavy book, she found herself eagerly anticipating the privilege of standing under their welcome shade—a privilege that she had never questioned at Chilton Manor. Her eyes wandered to the meadows. She glanced hastily about for a possible glimpse of her beloved Arabian. But she was nowhere in sight.

The wind gently blew the pale spring growth of the towering fruit trees beyond, causing Margaret to achingly remember her beloved Chilton Hall, once again, with its profusion of trees and the abundance of rhododendron in the meadows surrounding the manor. Intense homesickness washed over her as she gazed up into the trees' faint wash of color. With fresh determination welling up, she purposed to return to her homeland regardless of how long it took her to get there.

Remaining deep in thought, Margaret followed the castle wall— bordering the dry bed of a moat, reminding her that the castle had been surrounded by water at one time. She advanced to the rear of the fortress where she found the stone seat without difficulty. No one was in sight, so Margaret sat down beneath the pleasant boughs.

How was she to recognize the child Gavin? How old was he? Would his nurse accompany him for his lesson? Overhead, a wren chattered in the trees and the clouds parted to throw a brilliant warmth earthward. Her sudden overwhelming desire was to remain here among the living greenery. Margaret glanced back toward the village. Truly she would not return to the squalor of the village of Ballender—if not for Robin.

When Margaret turned her face from the village, she found herself face to face with Lord Ballender, who stood, looking at her from beneath a plum tree, hands on his hips. A well-tailored blue doublet complemented his lean, powerful build. He wore matching breeches and fitted stockings that emphasized his muscular body and broad shoulders. The man towering over her slender frame looked down into the clear cerulean eyes that focused on him.

"What are you doing here?" he demanded. "Where's Robin?"

"He's sick so he asked me to come in his place," she answered shortly, annoyed at his brusqueness.

The flashing cinnamon eyes probed Margaret's face as she gave her simple explanation. Lord Ballender's eyes focused with interest at the sun shining on the strands of golden hair peeping out from beneath her hooded cloak.

"Tell me," he said, lifting a brow. His mouth turned up in a wry twist on one side. "Why were you going to Corleal's a few weeks ago?"

"I am betrothed to him and I was going to my wedding."

Lord Ballender folded his arms in front of his vast chest and moved his feet apart. "He's a dolt and a fool. Why would you have wanted to marry such a man?" He hurried on, not giving her opportunity to answer. "Let me guess. Money? No. That's not it. You're not the kind who marries for money. Now what was the reason? Eh?"

His words angered her; yet the handsome man's presence was unsettling. She lifted her chin defiantly, staring straight ahead of her. "If your band of savages had not frightened our horses and caused my father's death on our way to the castle, I would be safe in England right now. But since I was the only one left, and defenseless, they took me captive instead of allowing me to continue on to Corleal Castle." She seethed with anger at the fresh recollection of the tragedy.

"Losing your father was regrettable, of course. But taking back your own possessions is hardly stealing, Miss Chilton."

"I, milord, am not one of your possessions!" She looked directly at the tall figure as he raised his brows and began circling slowly around her.

"Edward had his reasons."

Margaret said nothing. She stared ahead in dead silence. A sudden gust of wind took the cloak's hood from her hair and blew the cloud of softness about her wistful blue eyes.

"Your father insisted on settling his daughter in a prominent

51

family? Is that why you were marrying Corleal?" Lord Ballender watched her carefully while he questioned her. "You were obedient to your parents, weren't you? Hm? You Englishwomen are like that. No will of their own."

Margaret turned abruptly in an attempt to dart away. But he caught her and spun her about in time to see tears of hot anger making deep pools of her eyes.

Lord Ballender held her firmly and looked into the defiance burning on her face. "My arrows hit too close, did they?" His laugh rang out in the silence of their isolation. The corner of his mouth curved up to reveal a perfect set of white teeth in that ruggedly handsome face.

"So now I should ask your pardon? Eh? I ask pardon of no one and will not begin now." He pulled her roughly to his chest and savagely claimed her lips with his. For a moment, Margaret was too stunned with shock to move. But in the next instant, she jerked determinedly away from him and vent her fury at his boorish, uncouth behavior.

"Where's the boy I was sent here to teach?" she demanded. "I was told he'd be here when I arrived. I assume Gavin is your son so please bring him to me so we can begin." She spat the words out with tartness and then resumed. "Does your wife know that you kiss other women?" A stinging feeling of humiliation burned her face and she expected to be shaken instantly, without mercy, for that retaliatory statement.

Lord Ballender walked a few paces beyond where she stood. Without looking at her face he replied with carefully forced gravity, "Miss Chilton, I am not married and I don't plan to be. I have no son. *I* am Gavin, the pupil you are to teach. *I* intend to learn to read. And *you* are here to teach me. Is all that clear? Are you ready to begin?"

Margaret hesitated a moment before turning to face the handsome, neatly dressed nobleman standing with his hands looped casually behind him, gazing at her. "But why do you have the sudden desire to learn now? It is quite evident that you have never been so inclined before."

"I'll tell you the reason behind my desire for knowledge." He started to move about with great agitation, his chin rising fiercely. "You have no Regent who feels greater allegiance to France than to your country, do you?"

"No, milord."

"Nor are you pressed to pay tithes to a church that does nothing for you. You have no cursed fat French bishops, sitting on their backsides, doing nothing more than letting the churches fall to ruin and pilfering money from the poor to keep themselves in luxuries. Those tyrants demand killing taxes and drain our land of its wealth.

"We are overrun with Frenchmen and have a French Regent ruling us. Our land is no longer free," he stated heatedly, resuming the pacing. "But that will change. Soon. And when it does, I intend to be there and to be able to read and sign warnings and petitions. Our wretched foreign ruler won't listen to us; she listens to no one save her French advisors."

He breathed with fiery impatience rushing through his words. "The Scottish nobility and their wishes mean nothing to her. We no longer have any say in our own government. But we have a champion who will come soon to lead us. And when he does, Robin and I, along with all of Scotland, will be there to give him the support he'll need. We intend to rid ourselves of these French leeches even if it takes every last drop of our blood."

Gavin was breathing out fire as a dragon, his face burning with allegiance to the cause to which he had dedicated himself. "Recently one of our Scottish preachers was burned at the stake—by order of the Bishop of St. Andrews, that viper. When we placed a great pile of stones as a memorial and tribute to Walter Miln's death, the bishop ordered the stones to be taken down and used to repair his walls." Gavin continued to pace. "But that's going to change, too. I vow it. We'll have a national faith. And it won't be one foisted upon us by a wretched French Regent." His nostrils dilated with fury as he listed the grievances brought on by the French Regent and her counselors.

He bent down and angrily scratched the letters of the alphabet in the dirt at his feet and gave the sounds of each. Then he took the Bible from Margaret's hands and began to haltingly read a few words printed there.

"Where did Robin get this book?" Margaret asked, curiosity urging her to speak.

"From me. He saved my life a year ago and was wounded in the leg because of it. The Bible was a gift. As long as I can remember, Robin has talked of nothing but helping the people of Scotland. He has always wanted to learn to read, but he had no teacher." Lord Ballender's words suddenly became softer. "He believes God sent you to him, Margaret." Then with a glance toward her he added, "His description didn't do you justice, for he painted you in the likeness of a nun."

Margaret bit her lip and said nothing. She certainly had not considered that she or her disastrous situation could serve as a blessing from God. Perhaps God was using her to some good end. Perhaps she had been sent by him to help these Scots. And if God had it in his plan, she would be delivered to her betrothed—in God's own time.

For an hour, Margaret worked with the man, but his impatience stood in the way of his learning. Robin, in his slow determination, was a better student. But they shared the strong bond of desire.

Margaret walked back toward Robin's house, her mind whirling with confusion and conflicting emotions. She called to conscious thought the problems concerning the French Regent and her counselors. Who was this champion of whom Lord Ballender had spoken, and why hadn't he appeared before now? The time was definitely right for him to take charge of the whole unfortunate situation.

Her thoughts about the country's bitter problems were overshadowed, however, by a mental picture of the powerful build of young Lord Ballender, his flashing dark eyes and thick ebony hair, his carefully cropped beard and mustache. Sensations of his kiss still lingered on her lips, spawning waves of emotion she'd never experienced in her nineteen years. Her only other kiss—from Lord

Corleal—had been pressed lifelessly on her lips at the occasion of her formal betrothal to him. It had had no resemblance to that of Gavin Ballender.

A wave of rebuke washed in as a flood. "I *am* a betrothed woman, firmly promised to Lord Corleal," she reminded herself sternly. "I must guard against this kind of breach being repeated."

chapter

7

WHEN THE SUN CAST shadows across the ridge of the Cheviot Hills—the farthest peaks bathed in pale purple haze—a lone rider brought his stallion to a halt in front of the tailor's small house.

He slipped silently to the ground, a small parcel tucked securely under one arm. He tethered the horse to a post, and taking the present he'd brought with him, Lord Ballender headed directly for Robin's doorway, covering the distance with a few strides of his long, powerful legs. After a cursory knock, he pushed open the wooden door leading into the house. Gavin's eyes immediately surveyed the room and breathed in a surprisingly clean, fresh scent. His gaze sped to the pots and churn, spotless from obvious scouring. A faint smile touched his lips.

"How are you feeling, Robin?" Lord Ballender asked, turning toward the tailor. He walked directly to the bed of heather where the tailor lay with a linen sheet covering his slender frame. The glazed appearance of Robin's eyes denoted the illness that wracked his feverish body.

In answer to Lord Ballender's question, the tailor managed to get the words formed, but the response was labored and slow in coming. Robin turned his head toward the other man, closed his eyes in pain, and whispered through lips parched dry, "I wish I could say that I'm better, but I can't. I do have a good nurse, though."

"Where is she?" Gavin walked to the side of the room to place the parcel of fish on the old chest resting against the wall. "I brought you a herring for your supper," he added.

"Thank you, milord. My stomach isn't taking kindly to food, but Margaret will prepare it for Edward and herself. They will welcome it."

Lord Ballender seated himself on a heavy wooden chair by the fireplace. Before he could answer Robin, the door swung open and Margaret stepped into the house with a wooden bucket in her hand. Gavin fixed his eyes on her face as she set the pail on the floor and dipped some of the liquid into a pot. His forefinger rotated slowly but steadily across the neatly clipped mustache over his mouth.

When Margaret rose from her bent position, she moved toward Robin. Her pulse quickened when she saw Gavin, but she simply nodded a greeting to him, and with container in hand, went directly to Robin and knelt by his side. Her hands dipped into the water and squeezed out the cloth she had placed there, but no word passed from her lips.

The fire's amber glow on Margaret's features highlighted the delicately chiseled curves of her cheeks and lips, melting them into deep shadows on the far side of her face. Her hair reflected the flickering light of the fire as if it were spun from gold. Even the homespun dress attractively accentuated her well-proportioned figure.

As she worked, Margaret was fully aware that Lord Ballender was watching her, studying her. But she made certain her eyes never wandered from the task at hand. She recalled her secret devastation prompted by Lord Ballender's embrace. Even now, the same vivid sensations threatened to return and undermine her. His nearness caused an inner melting throughout her body. She still recalled the strength of his encircling arms and the pressure of his lips, firmly lowered against hers. In the silence of the room, Margaret thanked God she had work to occupy both her eyes and her fingers.

After a few moments, Gavin rose and commenced a steady pacing back and forth across the room before he spoke.

"I have word," he announced with deep irritation surfacing, "that the French soldiers and their families continue to pour like soup into the seaport at Leith even though our Scottish leaders have demanded the Regent put a stop to it."

The small seaport of Leith, Margaret had learned, was located about one mile from the inland town of Edinburgh and was used as a harbor for that town. Gavin's words caused her to picture French ships, white sails billowing in the stiff breezes from the chilling North Sea, maneuvering into the Firth of Forth to anchor along the quay. Arrogant French soldiers, uniforms sparkling, helmets glistening, would trip down the wooden planks with wives and children in tow, preparing to make their homes in this country they considered ripe for the plundering and conquering.

Lord Ballender's words portrayed his deeply coiled tension. "How convenient that we have a ruler who encourages the enemy to infiltrate our land! Even though Edinburgh is a distance, I wish to jump into the thick of activity against those contemptible leeches!" Gavin's voice gave vent to an inner explosion of anger. "We must force our cursed Regent to listen to us, Robin, and understand our situation. We *will not*, we *cannot*, give allegiance to this ruler when her interests are against our country. Our only remaining hope lies in help from England!"

"Our only hope is in God," answered Robin, conviction of his newfound faith rippling through his softly spoken words. "The poor are already groaning under the load of burdensome fees for weddings and burials. They can't stand under this overwhelming expense that's been put on them. The Regent and her clergy who bask in luxury have no conception of the struggles the common people of Scotland labor under. Only God can unite us and help us."

"What we need is a good strong army—and England's backing us up," Gavin asserted, defiance ringing strong in his voice—a tension taut as a wall ready to collapse.

"The people will perish unless our Maker intervenes and guides us," Robin said softly. Then as an afterthought he added, "Have you had word from the Scottish Brethren in the North?"

"Yes. The country is ripe, Robin. The burning of Walter Miln will unite us against such terrible acts. The Scottish leaders will realize that if we are to keep the vows of our Band, we must bestir ourselves to assure such a thing never happens again. No more sitting idly by. We must stand behind our other preachers—Willock, Methuen, Harlow, and Douglas—to the death. We must move with force in retaliation of this act—get the country solidly united.

"The Regent thinks she can do as she pleases and get away with it! We'll show her she can't! I've already sent word to the nobility in our southwestern area to meet at the Tolbooth as soon as we can set a date. The alternative to being completely overrun by French is an alliance with England—at least we'd have some backing against these blood suckers. The wealth we get when we overthrow the Regent will be all ours, Robin, as it should be." The last part of his vow was stated with firm determination.

"But," Robin warned weakly, "the poor must be our first consideration, milord. The preachers will need to be paid for their work as they go from village to town. We must unite under God first of all."

Margaret listened to the interchange of ideas between Robin and Gavin, shocked at what she heard, and coming more fully to a realization of what they actually faced.

Bound to the stake! Death by fire! The rallying cries against injustice began spreading like flames through a field of ripened grain. This latest barbaric act incited Scotsmen in all parts of the country to take issue with the Regent and her lieges. The cry became the rallying point for the inevitable approaching revolt. The murder created a new fervency against the French, fanning embers of anger and hatred to an intense white heat.

Margaret watched Robin climb the splintered steps up to the pulpit in the decaying stone church at Ballender and face those gathered for prayer and study. He decried—in a strong, undaunted voice—the savage burning of a faithful old man of God, Walter Miln.

"He was a just man!" Robin assured those assembled in the ancient church. "His only crimes in his advanced age were his faith in God and the sovereignty of Christ as the root of his hope, daring to answer in defense of his faith—that Christ is our sole mediator, not earthly men. He cried out against the injustices of the French and their immoral clergy! For this, Walter Miln was pronounced guilty of heresy and condemned to die by fire!"

Margaret sat on a small stool in the back of the crumbling church to listen. Robin's voice echoed around the thick stone pillars and reechoed from the vaulted ceiling overhead. Many at the gathering stood to listen. Others, like herself, had brought small stools, placing them haphazardly about the hard-packed earth beneath their feet so they could listen in relative comfort.

With interest, Margaret watched the reaction to Robin's words on the faces of the people congregated there. She marveled at how his reading had improved in the short time since he had given himself entirely to God. His eyes sparkled with enthusiasm as he told his listeners of God's love and forgiveness; a message of true hope—a different kind of news than they'd heard before. The truths were vibrant and alive: promises of peace and undying love from a God who cared. Robin's time had truly come and he was ready!

Although Margaret's ears were attuned to Robin's words, she was keenly aware of Lord Ballender's presence. Did Robin's message touch him at all? Surely he had a tender spot in his heart that could be softened by God's undying love. Margaret had difficulty controlling her eyes as she kept snatching occasional glances at him. His powerful legs were covered with amber hose and breeches. The sleeves and back of his emerald doublet were slashed in places, purposely allowing the gold lining to show through—Robin's handiwork. The whiteness of his gathered neck ruff made a stunning contrast to his black hair, beard, and mustache. His male vibrancy emanating from beneath the tanned skin of his face distinguished him—against the brightness of his ruff—set him apart from every man in the gathering. He was virile and compelling, unconsciously drawing her against her will.

Margaret forced her attention back to Robin's final words as he cited injustices that led to the inevitable breaking point. She was stunned to hear of the horrors that had preceded Walter Miln's murder.

"Paul Craw died," Robin recalled in a clear voice of purpose, "with a ball of brass forced in his mouth so he couldn't tell of his faith, in those last moments of his life. George Campbell, Adam Reid, Lady Polkeri—thirty persons in all—were brought before the archbishop and not one denied his faith. Patrick Hamilton endured a slow burning and suffered untold agony because of it, but called out his faith in Jesus Christ until the heat of the fire silenced him forever! From that day, burnings were conducted in a deep well, for, the archbishop claimed, these acts aided our cause!

"Many have risen to the cause and with the murdering of each, God has raised up another. Pray and study," exhorted Robin, "and be ready for the day when we will be free of our bondage! Victory will come, brethren, for it will be of God!"

When Robin finished speaking, Lord Ballender hurried forward to face the front row of burgesses—village merchants—without flinching, his face mirroring deep inner contempt.

"Our people in Edinburgh," he fumed, "have taken matters into their own hands to vent their anger against the rotten injustices we've taken from our Regent and cohorts. They took the wooden French patron saint from St. Giles Church and carried it to the North Loch and drowned it! Then they burned it! That act stirred up a hive of stinging rage among the Regent's bishops! And now," Gavin's face rose in triumph, "the Scottish leaders are summoned to Edinburgh in July! Aha! We will make it worth the woman's while, we will! No longer will we be stepped on like sniveling cowards!" Lord Ballender raised his arm in a bold gesture of defiance against the Regent who had promised at the death of her husband, the king of Scotland, to love his country. Then, with a surge of fury, Gavin shot the other arm into the air. "We'll fight!" he cried. "We'll fight to the death!"

With these triumphant words ringing in their ears, the people rose as one body. "Down with the French!" they chanted loudly in unison, gaining fiery momentum. "Down with the French!"

Margaret watched as the people took hold of the carved images of saints standing about the church, and in a great outpouring of anger, toppled them from their stands, until the last one lay at the base of the thick pillars that rose to the vaulted ceilings overhead. Margaret's hands flew to her mouth as she stood in stunned silence, her heart racing within.

"Down with the French!" The chant continued. "Down with the French!"

Watching the angry villagers, Margaret saw in the faces of those represented a vibrant dedication that chose freedom over bondage. No in-between.

What lies ahead?

chapter
8

To KEEP HER MIND off her homesickness, Margaret asked Robin to show her how to cut garments and construct them. She sat in Robin's small shop sewing the seams of a gray doublet when she heard a horseman clatter to a sudden stop in front of the house. He must be one of Robin's customers.

"Lord Ballender wants Robin and Margaret Chilton to be at the Tolbooth at sundown," was all he said. The man's simple, forthright command left no room for a negative response. Then, turning suddenly, the fellow left as quickly as he had arrived.

Margaret sighed and walked back to her sewing. Even though she couldn't come to a logical conclusion about the reason Lord Ballender would summon Robin and her at a place called Tolbooth, she had to admit that the idea of even this short trip was a welcome change from sitting in the dreary little house.

In answer to her query about an identification of the place to which they had been summoned, Robin replied, "The Tolbooth is the place where the village burgesses meet with Lord Ballender to make laws and solve problems. It also has the village jail beneath it."

The jail! "Why are we supposed to appear there?"

"No doubt it has to do with the French. Don't be afraid, Margaret. Lord Ballender has no intention of putting you in jail."

The sun was sinking along the horizon when Robin guided his horse toward the stone steps of the old Tolbooth, around which a number of horses were already tethered. He and Margaret made their way up to the wooden door, pushing it open into the large meeting room. Instead of finding the village burgesses inside, they were surprised to see a gathering of lords and gentlemen, of varying ages, with Lord Ballender.

Margaret was immediately aware of a restless stirring of anger and frustration among the assemblage. Although the presence of a woman in their midst caused mild curiosity, the hum of discontent never ceased as she and Robin were directed, by Gavin, to take seats in a darkened corner to the side of the room. He admonished them to be ready to read or write should they be called upon.

A rushlight taper in its small metal holder spread a bright glow on the somber faces of the bearded men, most of them older than Lord Ballender, seated around a heavy oak table in the center of the room. From the place Margaret sat with Robin, she could see chisled features and handsomely made doublets bathed in deep shadows, a stark contrast to the bright illumination covering the faces on the opposite side of the table.

"I have in my hand," Lord Ballender cut into the murmur of conversation, "a copy of the petition the nobles in other parts of Scotland intend to announce at Mercat Crosses as soon as they are signed. Please listen to it." He stood straight and tall. The flickering brightness of the light formed flashing slivers of light to glisten in the cinnamon depths of his eyes as he read the contents slowly, painstakingly to the end.

Margaret was acutely aware of the amount of time he'd spent laboring over those words before he had come tonight. She realized how determined he was in his purpose. Few of the noblemen represented by their presence this night could do as well, if they could read at all.

When he finished, Gavin looked up. "Those who sign this will unquestionably band themselves together against the French menace facing us and the Roman religion foisted on us against our will. You're well aware, as I am, that we've been patient far too long!" Another murmuring of agreement rippled through the assembly.

"The Regent and her cohorts call us heretics!" Gavin's voice thickened in anger as he continued. "They labeled us such for rebelling against the bishops and priests. We're heretics because our preachers want an undefiled, simple faith to live by.

"The Regent claims she knew nothing of Walter Miln's burning," he added with disdain. "Rubbish! We will, by the signing of this petition," he stated boldly, "announce to the Regent and her counselors that we will *not* accept their miserable treatment of us any longer. This document will declare plainly, at every Mercat Cross in Scotland, our rebellion against their actions."

The rushlight flickered on the bearded faces of the men gathered about the table as they prepared to sign the document. Lord Ballender's nostrils dilated as a fire-breathing dragon and his eyes flicked sparks as bright as a blacksmith's anvil.

"Either make a complete commitment with the Brethren or make no commitment at all and be counted with the damnable French!" Gavin's words burst with fiery conviction as he grasped a quill, and in large deliberate letters, wrote his name below the last word of the document. Passing the parchment to the other signers seated around the table, he stood silently, expectantly, to watch.

Margaret sensed that one of the men held back, apparently counting the complete cost of such an act.

"We have nothing to lose," reminded one of the nobles, "but the threat of becoming a French province under this despicable Regent."

The man hesitated no longer. He signed.

Chilling gusts of wind moved about the Tolbooth as the noblemen, Margaret, and Robin descended the stone steps to their waiting horses. Before they had a chance to mount, they heard Gavin's sharp cry.

Instantly, all eyes shifted toward the direction in which he faced. Red-orange streaks flared upward into the dusky sky. Shrouds of billowing smoke blanketed flames beneath, telling onlookers that houses and stores of grain were being gutted and ravaged in the village nearest Ballender. Two of the men mounted in haste and

CAPTIVE'S PROMISE

sped toward the bridge and their homes that lay in the direction of the devastating blaze.

Villagers began pouring from their homes and from the alehouse to see what the commotion signified.

The lean figure of Lord Ballender was in his saddle, his horse whinnying and making agitated movements on the cobblestone pavement. Gavin watched the flames mounting steadily into the darkening blue of the night sky.

Catching the flanks of his horse with his heels, he moved his edgy black stallion toward Robin. "Be on the alert," he warned everyone, "for that raiding party might try to circle around here and take us by surprise. The soldiers at the castle will be ready to take to the fields, for they've seen the blaze by now. We need our cattle and horses for the coming revolt and we'll not give them up to a band of cursed Englishmen!"

As men gathered around, Edward pushed close to Gavin, eager for orders to ride. "Cursed English," he hissed. "Can it be that fool, Corleal, creating this havoc?"

"Watch your words, brother," advised Robin. "We may need those English fools, as you call them, to help us rout the French from our shores before long."

Margaret's heart raced within her and she clenched her teeth in anger at the loose words of Lord Ballender. Was Lord Corleal really searching for her? With hope soaring, she unconsciously moved forward, studying the flaming inferno in the darkening sky. Her pulse quickened at the prospect of being rescued. She longed for the face of a familiar rider who could set her free and carry her back across the border to her beloved England.

In her eager anticipation of rescue, Margaret raced forward toward the river until a black stallion dashed across her path, halting her.

"You're going nowhere!" Lord Ballender's sharp words flashed from atop his mount. Then looking to the tailor he ordered tersely, "Robin! Take Margaret to the castle and leave her there!"

Before she could spin about and cry out against the injustice of

68

his command in stern protests, Margaret saw him wheel around, dig his heels into the horse's sides, and shout to Edward.

"Come on! We'll head for the rise beyond us and see what this is all about!"

Robin hurried forward, calling out a command to obedience. "No, Margaret. You can't be certain it's your Lord Corleal out there. Many raids are made across these borders from spring until autumn. And if it isn't Lord Corleal, himself, riding in, who would recognize you? I wouldn't want to be standing in your shoes if a band of wild men came dashing into the village and you ran to them willingly. They wouldn't likely believe you. Margaret, consider your situation. You are safe with us here, so let well enough alone. In time you will get back to your Lord Corleal, but for now, we truly need you here."

Margaret turned away from Robin, her eyes smarting with tears, her sudden ray of hope dissolving before her eyes. The compassion she held for the tailor was great—and she understood the grave circumstances facing him and his countrymen—but the choice between Robin and Lord Corleal's rescue was no choice at all.

She purposely shoved both Robin and Lord Ballender far from her mind as she pleaded inwardly from a deep reservoir of anguish, *Lord, help me! Show Lord Corleal where I am. Lead him to me and let me be taken away from here!*

chapter
9

MARGARET WATCHED the racing figures of Edward and Lord Ballender disappear into the engulfing darkness, her mind reeling from the terse order flung to Robin as they left. Swinging numbly toward the tailor, her face blanched white, she appealed to him. "Will I be put in a dungeon, Robin?" she asked fearfully. The constriction threatened to choke the words from her mouth.

"Lord Ballender would never do that to you." His answer was softly confident. He took a small rush, lighted it from one of the men's lanterns, and touched it to the rush taper in his own lantern. When the fire burned brightly, he limped, with the aid of his crutch, to the horse tethered at the stone column. Motioning for Margaret to climb onto the waiting mount, he handed her the lantern to hold for him until he was seated. When she was perched reluctantly on the horse's back, she again voiced her concern for the uncertain fate awaiting her.

"For what reason does he want me placed in the fortress if he does not intend to make me a prisoner?" she pursued, believing the situation both inconceivable and unfair.

"To keep you from being taken away by raiders, Margaret."

She wanted to cry out her wish to have no part of Ballender Castle—far preferring the raiders, if they were Lord Corleal's men. But she was aware that Robin was simply acting on orders from Lord Ballender. Regardless of the tailor's encouraging words, she remained convinced Lord Ballender would put her exactly where he wanted her. She turned her face momentarily toward the distant flames and then fearfully shifted her gaze toward the dark, formidable outline of the castle looming above the village of Ballender, its façade dimly illuminated by the brilliant flames lighting the night sky.

As Margaret and Robin approached the fortress, they glimpsed the soldiers on their mounts, dashing from the great castle gate, their long spears pointing straight ahead in preparation for possible trouble. As Robin identified himself to the guard at the gatehouse, Margaret's eyes were unconsciously drawn upward to the portcullis, a strong iron grating hanging in readiness to block the entrance of Ballender Castle to invaders.

But to Margaret, the frightful pointed teeth at its base seemed a threat, rather than a mere fortification. Instead of protecting her from enemy raiders, they would serve to shut out her only means of escape—her only route to Lord Corleal, and to the life she so longed to have. They passed beneath the jagged structure and moved on.

Robin cautiously avoided the onrushing troops as he urged his horse across the large barmkin—courtyard—to the towerhouse on the far side of the enclosure. Margaret's eyes traveled to a lantern hanging above the towerhouse door, lighting the steps of a high stone stairway leading into the castle interior.

"Miss Chilton is to be kept at the castle," Robin called to the guards at the towerhouse. "Lord Ballender's orders."

Margaret gazed fearfully about her. High curtain walls were topped with the crenels and merions—alternating open and fortified walls—of the battlements. The crenelations connected formidable corner towers whose pointed caps rose high and sharp into the sky.

Robin maneuvered to the stone stairway, then reached up to help Margaret dismount. For a moment she scanned the tailor's face before she spoke.

"I—I will miss you," she admitted, trying to hold back a rush of tears. Margaret drew in her bottom lip, gnawing on it as her eyes continued to search Robin's face. "Your kindness has meant much to me," she asserted thickly.

Robin gave her a comforting smile. "This is not good-by, Margaret. Both Lord Ballender and I have need of more lessons in reading and writing and we have naught but you to teach us." Placing his hand gently on her arm, he added hastily, "I will pray for you every day. God's grace sent you here, for without you, I could never have found the great abiding peace I have in my heart." The corners of his lips thrust upward still further. "Come," he urged. "Smile. Everything will be well."

The tears that had been pooling near the surface of Margaret's eyes now broke into little streams of salty liquid and trickled down her face. Despite them, she forced a smile. "I will pray for you, too," she whispered.

"Now," Robin observed, glancing at the doorway flooded with lantern light from above, "the steward is waiting for you. You have my promise that he will take good care of you while you are in the castle."

Margaret nodded. She proceeded up the steps to the doorway, then lingered a moment before entering. "Robin," she called urgently, turning toward the tailor as he climbed with painful effort onto his horse, "will you please bring my dresses, comb, and soap?"

"Early on the morrow," he promised, giving a positive nod. Margaret gazed wistfully across the barmkin, her eyes following Robin on his way toward the gatehouse. Then, with rising apprehension, she swung around to face the steward of Ballender Castle.

The man was tall. His lean, muscular body was clothed in a deep blue doublet matching his fitted hose and breeches. The flickering rushlight he held in front of him rendered his face dark and brooding as he considered the young woman who stood before him.

O God, deliver me from this frightful place, was Margaret's silent plea. No matter Robin's encouraging words to the contrary, she

73

anticipated at the next moment to be roughly snatched and thrown into a dark, damp cell to await her fate, whatever it might be. Fear shone in her eyes as she surveyed the man in front of her, his momentary indecisiveness seeming interminable.

Wordlessly the steward motioned her through the high arches of the Great Hall, and toward a dark circular tower. Stone steps, a part of the wall, wound upward in the flickering light, appearing eerie, grotesque, and cold. The man who climbed before her probably considered her a criminal.

When, at last, they reached the third level, the steward moved quickly ahead to open a heavy oak door leading into a large vaulted room. Continuing in silence, he moved directly to a carved chest and lit the rush taper already perched on an adjustable, metal-toothed holder. "I'll send you a little water," were his only words before he produced a key and, with a cursory nod of his head, locked the door behind him.

Margaret's heart sank to her feet with the grating sound of that lock. "I am now a prisoner," she whispered fearfully, "in a fortified keep with little hope of escape." Closing her eyes, Margaret leaned back heavily against the cold stone wall, alone and discouraged. *No, not alone,* she told herself. *God knows where I am — and he cares.*

Paul, too, was imprisoned, Margaret reminded herself in her agony, but he made the best of it. Not only did he make the best of his situation, he sang songs. *O Lord,* she breathed silently, *if I must make the best of my captivity, please help me, for I have no stomach for any of these unbearable circumstances.* Paul may have sung, but Margaret could not summon the fortitude to do likewise. Only God's grace could keep her from becoming bitter and truly beaten down.

She found small comfort in the fact that her confinement wasn't in the dreaded subterranean cell she had feared. For this, a tight little sigh of relief and thanksgiving escaped her mouth. She discovered a real bed—its mattress stuffed with down—instead of a pile of heather on the floor. In comparison to the stone hut of the tailor and his brother, this chamber was actually rather a pleasant place.

Slipping off her shoes, Margaret lay down on the mattress. The rope supports of the bed frame and the feather softness felt heavenly after the crude matting of heather on which she had grown accustomed to sleeping. But she already missed Robin. Who else would care enough to talk to her and render her dreaded imprisonment a little less hurtful?

No Bible would be found here—nor anything else to occupy her time. The hours promised to drag endlessly. *Why has Lord Ballender put me here? Or is Lord Corleal truly to blame for this humiliating captivity? Could I really be worth the price of a ransom?*

Within moments, a servant girl with an extra rush taper and water appeared at the door. A shy little thing clad in a coarse, woolen homespun gown dyed a dull nut-brown, she silently completed her assigned duties. As she turned to leave without saying a word, Margaret asked, "May I please have a fire, a pot for heating water, a little soap, and a towel for bathing?"

A mixture of curiosity and disdain spread across the pale little face, as the maid's eyes flicked over Margaret's garments, as coarse and plain as her own. She hesitated a moment before responding. "I will ask Master Campbell," she finally conceded, before scurrying from the room as if she were a mouse pursued by a cat. Her hand pulled the heavy door shut behind her.

When again she was alone, Margaret continued her survey. Stone walls swept up to a high ceiling, cross-beamed with heavy oak timbers. A tapestry of a country scene hung on one wall. Over the four intricately carved bed posts were curtains and a canopy of heavy gold damask, embroidered with flowing scrolls of crimson silk thread. Two Flemish chairs flanked the fireplace. The bulky oak chest against the far wall was covered with an ornate series of cunningly carved figures.

Built into the thickness of one of the castle walls, Margaret found a small room furnished with a sturdy Flemish table covered with an embroidered carpet of bright threads, and two chairs arranged as if for visitors. What irony! But the sobering thought crossed her mind that perhaps these rooms were only temporary quarters—her next move could be to a much less comfortable station. Margaret sighed and wandered back to the fireplace in search of a tinder box to start a fire and relieve the room of its dampness.

Before she found what she sought, the door swung open and the little maid brought in the requested articles. The girl placed the water on the chest, then knelt to kindle a fire in the fireplace, using dried chunks of peat.

Left alone once more, Margaret moved toward the bowl of warm water to wash her face and hands. As she was drying with the towel, Margaret again heard the key turning in the locked door. Believing it to be the servant returning for the dirty water, she didn't bother to look up—until Lord Ballender's voice broke the silence.

"Are you comfortable?" he asked, striding into the room and coming to a standstill next to her by the fireplace.

"Do you always walk into rooms without knocking?" she demanded. She'd not be treated as if her quarters were a public thoroughfare!

"Whenever it suits me."

"Why am I here?" Margaret asked, refusing to cower before him in her inquiry about her imprisonment. "I am locked in here as a common thief or criminal. I haven't done anything."

"This room is hardly a cell," he commented dryly, raising an arched brow at her statement. "The reason is obvious. I wanted you safe."

"I was safe enough with Robin," she objected, turning away from him. Margaret wrapped her arms tightly about herself to relieve the agitation of her circumstances.

Gavin moved forward, placing his hands boldly on her shoulders and swinging her around to face him. For a moment he stared into her startled eyes. "You are here, Margaret, because I want you here." His answer was clipped and final.

Immediately Margaret put up her hands to ward off a possible embrace. She refused to submit to that humiliating experience a second time.

Ignoring her attempt at release, Gaving continued to grasp her shoulders firmly in his strong hands. He had no smile on his lips, no hint of amused mockery in his face when his eyes searched hers.

"Margaret," he asked, closely studying her reaction, "why do you wait with such stubbornness for that fool Corleal?"

"Because we are betrothed." Her retort was quick and simple, without a trace of apology for either her actions or her situation.

"This marriage was arranged, wasn't it." Gavin's words were more a statement of fact than a question.

"What difference does it make, milord? I am promised. That's the way the situation will remain until I can return to him. Now," she insisted, turning away and simultaneously attempting to push away from his rock-hard chest, "please leave."

Lord Ballender's strong forefinger forced her chin upward so her blue eyes met the sparkle in his dark brown eyes. "And if he should reject you because you love someone else . . ."

"That, milord," Margaret defensively and definitely assured him, "will not happen."

Gavin's flashing black eyes, reflecting the flames from the fire, seared into her heart, causing it to beat erratically. She resolved anew that not one flicker of emotion would betray the turmoil within.

Gavin moved back. He snatched his mantle and flung it casually over one shoulder with a flick of his wrist. Then pivoting about he added, smiling, "Sleep well, my love."

Before she could hurl her objection to the familiar term, he pulled the door shut behind him and turned the key securely in the lock. In the quiet of the somber staircase beyond, she heard Gavin race down the steps, whistling a strange melody that soon trailed away into nothingness in the stillness of the room. Margaret's hands unclenched from their tight knots, but her mind refused to release the picture of a teasing smile on a handsome face.

chapter
10

As THE EARLY LIGHT OF MORNING filtered through one long, narrow window into the castle chamber, Margaret opened her eyes. But she hardly saw her surroundings. Instead she pictured her father, Lord Corleal, Robin, the French, Lord Ballender—all a great jumble of confusion not easily sorted out nor understood.

Margaret's life had taken a drastic turn from the straight, well-ordered plan that had proceeded from childhood until her capture by the reivers and her arrival at Ballender. Now, each day began and ended with uncertainty. With a sigh, she pushed back the woolen blanket and sheet and rose from her bed.

After splashing her face with water, she tidied her bed, dressed, then tugged her fingers through her thick blond hair to make a stab at neatness out of complete disorder. Hopefully, Robin would bring her comb to her today.

Margaret's eyes moved studiously over the rough stone surfaces that gradually slanted away from the window, down into the room where she stood. She judged the thickness of the walls to be about eight cubits. But even if she could manage to climb the slant and squeeze to the window, she knew signaling was in vain; she could not be seen from so great a height.

A light knock and the familiar grating of the key in the lock announced the arrival of the same serving girl who had attended her the night before. "Lord Ballender wishes to see you in the Great

Hall, Miss." With a wag of her head, the girl withdrew and headed back down the stairway, leaving the chamber door ajar behind her.

The unlocked door represented at least a small show of Lord Ballender's intentions to give her a token freedom. Margaret's spirit rose with that thought. Spiraling down to the Great Hall, she ran her fingers desperately through her matted hair once more. She must look tidy before—the servants.

The Great Hall door was standing open when she set foot on the threshold of the cavernous room. "You rise early," Lord Ballender commented with amusement from his carved chair at the head of the table. "I suppose you are hungry? Eh? Come. Breakfast with me." His hand reached over to grasp the heavily carved chair to his right and pull it toward him.

Margaret moved forward to the chair he had arranged for her, noting the high ceiling fortified with mammoth arched beams. At each end was a high window—the only openings to allow light into the huge room. Beyond the table was a monstrous tapestry, its size proportionate to the magnitude of the chamber, depicting a hunt scene embroidered with many bright colors to enliven the white wall with a splash of vivid brightness. To the rear of the head chair was a stone fireplace.

"What is to become of me here? I can't bear to be imprisoned for reasons unknown to me."

"But you're not a prisoner," Gavin insisted. "As of today, you may wander at will."

"Wandering does not suit me. I have been accustomed to keeping my hands busy. Is there some task I can do in the castle to pass my time until—"

"Until?" He interrupted Margaret. His eyebrows shot up in response to her reference. No smile formed on his lips.

"Until I am rescued," she answered. Her tone was flat and firm.

Lord Ballender chose to ignore her reference to her rescue, saying in a tone of dismissal, "If you need a task assigned to you, I will speak to my steward about it." He leaned forward and broke off a piece of freshly baked bread, motioning as he did so, for her to take the seat next to him.

She glanced at the food he handed her and at him as he tore, animal-like, into his portion of the crusty loaf. Silently she lowered her head a moment, asking God's blessing on the food.

Her eyes snapped open in midprayer, when Lord Ballender, in a violent motion that frightened his breakfast companion, stabbed the knife into the meat on the platter so the handle pointed straight in the air.

"That won't make the food taste any better," he commented, leaning back in his chair and casually crossing his ankle over his knee. "What is the purpose of the prayer?" He cut a large slice of beef, again spearing it with his knife, but holding it steady. Shifting his gaze in a manner of assessment, he waited for her reply.

"I am thankful for any and all blessings."

"Oh?" he mocked, his mouth twisting into a challenging grin. "You believe that your being here is a blessing, do you?"

"God knows where I am," she answered calmly. *I truly believe that,* she told herself, though she could not pretend to know God's reasons for bringing her here. Nevertheless, she would trust him to be her comfort and stay until her rescue and return to England.

"Robin speaks highly of you," Lord Ballender offered, along with the slice of meat. "He, too, professes a trust in the mystery of God."

"It's no mystery. Nor is it a secret. God will dwell in any heart that invites him in." Her eyes strayed his way as she gave the quiet explanation, and accepted the beef with a nod of thanks.

"Not in mine," interjected Gavin. "I've managed very well on my own."

"Perhaps you would be surprised to find that God manages better still."

Gavin deftly changed the subject. "My orders are that you be unhindered by confinement. But," he stressed, pointing his meat-laden knife at her, "I must warn you that we have many soldiers posted here. Some are single men who will be—let's say—attracted to a bonny maiden with golden hair, and especially, one who is unwed."

Margaret felt the heat of embarrassment rising in her neck and face in spite of willing it otherwise. "As a woman promised in marriage, I will not find that a problem," she assured him, refusing to back down.

Lord Ballender smiled and picked up his large pewter cup in one hand, taking a long draught before offering it to Margaret. For a moment she hesitated, studying Gavin Ballender curiously. Until now, Margaret hadn't been fully aware of his even white teeth nor of his hair curling slightly at the edges.

He continued to hold forth his cup, despite her hesitation. "It's not poisonous," Gavin snapped in irritation.

Margaret couldn't tell him that she had recalled her father, a look of love on his face, offering her mother his cup in the same way.

"I know. It's not that—" Margaret's face flushed pink, and in her embarrassed confusion, in accepting the offered cup, her fingers came in accidental contact with the warmth of his hand. She felt her heart race to that simple touch, and touching her lips to the same cup that had, just moments earlier, touched his, left her more than a little unsettled.

When Margaret saw Gavin wipe his hands on a towel, signaling the meal was completed, she rose and neatly arranged the remaining food on the platter before placing it on the linen-covered serving table for the little maid to remove.

Suddenly she felt his hands on her shoulders, and the warmth of his touch caused her, ironically, to be frozen in place. In spite of her attempts to pull away, he held her firmly.

"Your hair smells as sweet as blooming heather in autumn, Margaret," he whispered softly, breathing dangerously close to her ear. "It's very bonny."

She could not submit to his enticing words! She managed to pull away and walk a few steps toward the fireplace, asking in a tone she hoped did not betray her errant emotions, "It was Lord Corleal searching for me last night?"

"More than likely. But he'll look in vain if ever he comes to Ballender."

By July the winds had shifted and rain was frequent. But in spite of it, Robin continued preaching in villages and towns round about Ballender. He had told Margaret, on one of his infrequent visits, that Lord Ballender backed him, gave him protection and, as a result, caused Robin to be numbered as one of the rebel preachers. His speaking out had resulted in his being branded an outlaw—put to the horn—by the Regent in the royal capital of Edinburgh. Regardless, Robin refused to stop.

The people of southwest Scotland welcomed his words as a parched land welcomes rain and soaks up every drop. Long without spiritual food except for the bungling efforts of illiterate, disinterested vicars, they flocked to homes and openly met in the decayed, half-used churches around Ballender. Throughout Scotland, public manifestos were read at market crosses: "We denounce the French-backed religion and declare ourselves enemies to it." The cause against French domination shot forward—like a cannonball—with fresh enthusiasm and determination.

Daily, Margaret climbed the winding stone stairway early in the morning to follow the walkway around four sides of the battlements. She peered through the deep cut crenelations down on the village to the north, in hopes of a glimpse of Robin riding toward the sandstone bridge, with three or four assigned soldiers for protection against sudden attackers or French agitators. At the sight of him, she raised her hand and whispered softly, "Godspeed. You have so much hope to give, so much joy to share," continuing her watch until he crossed the bridge and disappeared from view beyond the farthest hazy, gorse-patched hill. Then she would turn and make her way to the servant's hall for her assigned day's work.

The rain began, cold and bleak, early one morning, but Margaret climbed the stone stairs and stood at the doorway onto the battlements, despite it, to watch for Robin. The smoke rising above the great kitchen chimney billowed in the thick gray mists above. Margaret leaned her head against the musty cold stones and brushed the blinding mist from her eyes, determining afresh not to crumple in despair. If only she were not a virtual prisoner in Ballender Castle, she would now be Lady Corleal, safely married, well settled into her routine and life, and perhaps with a child on the way.

Surely God had a purpose in all this. She had to believe that he did.

By midmorning the rain ceased, the clouds parted, and a bright wash of sunlight spread over Ballender. Margaret took a stool and made her way beyond the towerhouse door to a place near the bottom step where she sat, quite alone, with three new dresses in her lap, each of a coarse fabric befitting a servant at the castle.

As she pushed her needle through the material to form hems, Margaret's thoughts drifted to her own lovely gowns, especially her wedding garments. The beautiful silks and velvets had been her personal treasures. Never in her wildest dreams had she imagined that one day she would be sitting near a castle step in Scotland, dressed in the plain, simple garment of a servant, and sewing gowns for the serving girls of a castle. .

What had become of her possessions? Could Lord Ballender have stored them in the castle? Or had he given them away? A long, drawn-out sigh escaped her lips.

"Lay not up for treasures for yourselves upon the earth, where thieves dig through and steal," Margaret whispered softly to herself as she worked, "but lay up treasures for yourselves in heaven." Her treasure of garments had disappeared, but the treasure of God's love was still tucked safely away in her heart where no border reivers or nobleman could ever take them away.

Poor Father, she reminisced. She was newly thankful he had insisted she learn the duties of a large household and understand how to perform household tasks. If it were not for her ability to sew, she would be idly passing the time in a tower room, a virtual prisoner to her own incapability. Again she drew in her breath and let it out slowly. *Poor Father,* she repeated in her heart. His life had ended so abruptly that he was unaware of his fate.

So deep in thought was Margaret that she neither saw nor heard Lord Ballender running lightly down the steps until he came to a halt beside her.

"You lost no time in finding something to do," he commented with a grin, studying the careful stitches she made in the coarse cloth. "It is not necessary that you do that."

"I'm aware of that, milord." Instead of belaboring her need to work, she determined to question him about what end had come to her belongings. "Are my horse and my gowns at the castle?"

"Yes. They're all here." He made no offer to fetch them; nor did he explain further.

At least she knew that they were in his keeping.

"My mare is well?" She kept her eyes on her work, careful not to let them stray to the man standing beside her.

"Of course."

"She won't be sold or mistreated?" Her voice took on a thickness engendered by the remembrance of her faithful mount.

Lord Ballender's response was curt. "What makes you think she would?"

"What of my dresses?"

"They're safe." He tossed her the casual response over his shoulder. His eyes were on the groom bringing his horse from the stable.

"I was afraid . . ."

"That you no longer had wedding garments?" He moved a few steps nearer her, and placed his hands on his rust-colored woolen breeches. "Get rid of your wedding dresses? Why would I? You will need them when you marry!"

He shoved his foot into the stirrup, swung a leg over the stallion's back, and both rider and mount shot off across the barmkin.

chapter
11

For an hour or more, Margaret continued with her sewing—until a rider galloped into the barmkin and headed straight for the towerhouse entrance where she was sitting.

"Master Campbell is here, Miss?"

"He's inside," she answered him, but immediately returned her gaze to her needle. His lascivious stare sent an involuntary shudder along her spine before he silently moved up the steps and was ushered into the towerhouse. Why would he give her such a look? Suddenly, crystal-clear, she understood. Her occupancy of one of the finest rooms at the castle, her presence at Lord Ballender's own table, had been misinterpreted. *Oh, no!* Her face flushed crimson. The servants and townspeople must believe her to be immoral—the mistress of the lord of the castle.

She looked quickly around her, taking in all the activity in the courtyard: stable boys cleaned the stables, stonemasons chipped at blocks of fine ashlar in preparation for repairing a window frame, and a smith shod a horse. From inside the castle came the monotonous sound of a little maid pounding sugar from a huge, rock-hard loaf. No, surely she was wrong. No one seemed the least bit curious about her; no one gave her even a cursory glance. Yet . . .

Margaret rose, carrying the gown on which she was working, and made her way across the barmkin to the gate-house. At the cavernous entranceway, she gazed beyond the sharp teeth of the portcullis overhead to the moors.

I am a prisoner, no matter what Lord Ballender says! If only she could walk in the fields or race her Arabian through the far hills. But her privileges ceased at the castle gate.

When the aromas of boiled meat reached her nose, Margaret made her way to the kitchen to ask Master Campbell if he would permit her to sit at the table with the servants in their dining area on the lower floor. Perhaps that would keep her from the gossipmongers of Ballender castle.

Margaret found the steward descending the winding stairs. She immediately approached him. But before she could form a question, he spoke to her as his foot touched the bottom step.

"Milord left instructions for you to have your midday meal served in the Hall, Miss Chilton," he informed her.

"No, thank you." Her return was instantaneous. "I'll eat with the servants in the kitchen." Margaret's chin protruded a fraction and her eyes looked directly at the steward, leaving no question as to her determination in this matter.

The steward's brows rose slightly. He cast her a quizzical look. "Very well," he conceded.

With the approach of the midday meal, Margaret made certain she appeared in the servant's hall in order to help carry the food to the table before the servants gathered. She resolved to spend as little time with Lord Ballender as possible until . . . what?

O Lord, she pleaded silently as she carried a platter of bread to the table, *how long must I wonder at my fate? How long must I remain confined inside these castle walls?*

After the meal was finished, and before Margaret again took up her sewing, she slipped quietly from the room and walked up the steps to her chamber. Immediately her eyes fell upon her clothes, lying on her bed. With eager fingers, Margaret picked up the comb and ran it through her unkempt hair before she continued up the stone stairway to the walkway along the battlements.

The magnificent view left her breathless. Margaret moved closer to the powerful stone battlement and leaned against it. In all directions white puffs of cloud formed patterns, shifting each moment into new formations. A sudden movement, so slight she might have easily missed it, caught her eye. A small brown sparrow sat in her snug little nest in the cracks of the mortar between two stones of the round tower.

With few trees in sight, the little feathered animal had chosen the next best site for her hiding place. *If God is mindful of this tiny sparrow,* she reasoned, *surely he cares for me, too.* An added measure of assurance crept into her heart.

With a shift of her eyes to the sandstone bridge, Margaret's focus was drawn to two riders galloping down the main street of Ballender toward the castle: the one, Lord Ballender; the other, a young woman—her hair, dark as chestnuts; her back, straight as the high-backed chair in the Great Hall. She sat proudly on her gray mount, her face beautiful, with an air of assurance in her black eyes that was echoed in the set of her mouth.

From her hidden vantage point, Margaret saw Lord Ballender and the woman dismount. A broad smile creased the new arrival's mouth as she hopped lightly to the ground. In moments, both she and Lord Ballender entered the castle and disappeared from view.

Margaret leaned over the low wall to watch the activity in the barmkin below. The servants carried bags of oats from the barn, the smith made sparks with his hammer, and an old man threw handfuls of grain through the slats of the chicken cages. Though her eyes focused on the movement below, her awareness encompassed only Lord Ballender and the woman with whom he had arrived moments before.

She drew herself up, circling the battlement, the young woman's radiant smile foremost in her thoughts. The wounding prick of jealousy that pierced her heart was sharp as a sword, something she was loath to admit. Never, before coming to Scotland, had she experienced such an uncomfortable reaction as this. *Lord, help me,* she breathed heavenward.

When the supper hour approached, Margaret returned to the kitchen for her meal, not bothering to ask the steward's permission. She could not submit to eating with Lord Ballender. Margaret was glad she'd made her decision earlier in the day, for it wouldn't appear as if her determination were prompted by the appearance of the dark-haired woman in the company of the man.

The platters of steaming food were being carried up the stone stairway for the table in the Great Hall. Obviously Lord Ballender had a guest for supper.

"Miss Chilton," the steward motioned impatiently, turning momentarily from the inspection of the chickens roasting on the spit at the fireplace and interrupting her thoughts, "Lord Ballender is waiting supper for you in the Hall." The curt command gave her no choice in the matter.

Margaret opened her mouth to object, but decided it would be better to explain her reservations about sitting at Lord Ballender's table to him alone. She gave the steward a cursory nod of her head, and moved to her purpose, much as she dreaded it—much as she dreaded seeing his guest.

Gavin stood by the fireplace with his hands clasped behind him while the servants placed his meal on the table. One girl poured wine into his cup, another cut the fowl apart. But there was no evidence of a guest—no pretty dark-haired girl at his table or standing beside him. On Margaret's appearance he turned about with his back to the fireplace, his feet resting in a wide stance. Beams from the wall lantern mirrored the sparkle in the black depths of each eye.

"I hear that you have thrown yourself into working with the servants and that you insist on eating your meals with them in the servants' hall. Why?"

"In answer to both questions, I want to keep occupied, and I prefer not to eat alone with you. It's improper." Her intention was to make her position clear as spring water. She folded her hands at arm's length in front of her, adding, "I want no cause for whisperings among the servants about my conduct or presence here."

"For my part, it's proper," Gavin declared firmly. "I happen to like company when I eat and I like yours. Now please sit down, Margaret, for I'm famished and I want to eat my supper before it cools and the fat congeals on the meat."

Margaret's thoughts unconsciously slipped back to his earlier companion. If he wanted company, why didn't he invite *her* to supper? Exactly what did the young woman mean to him? She acquiesced to his wishes, but not without qualms.

Immediately Lord Ballender dismissed the servants and then turned to Margaret. With a crooked twist of his mouth he warned, "Your prayer had best be quick, for I will wait but a few seconds to begin eating." With an impatient flick of his finger, he motioned her to begin.

A little smile turned up the corners of her mouth as she said her short prayer. "Are you always so impatient?" she asked, casting a hasty glance at him. She moved her chair a little farther away.

"Yes." Then he chuckled at the obvious movement of her seat. Reaching for a chicken leg, he handed it to Margaret before taking one for himself. "This is the first time I have seen you smile," he observed with interest, his voice growing softer. "It is lovely."

The conversation was taking a turn with which Margaret was less than pleased, so she sought to change the subject. "How is Robin? I haven't seen him for a few days."

"Busy. He's been preaching in churches all over this part of Scotland. And the people still flock to hear him. But, as you know, the Regent has outlawed Robin—as she has all of the other preachers who are going about, preparing the people, uniting them for our cause."

"Is he in any danger?"

"Not with my soldiers accompanying him. The miserable Regent would like to kill all our preachers as she did Walter Miln. But she'll not touch Robin!" His brow knitted in a determined frown, his eyes narrowing to mere slits.

He enlarged on the circumstances facing them. "The preachers have been ordered to appear in Edinburgh, along with the nobility, to answer charges about the North Loch incident in June as well as the movement and speaking activities of our preachers."

Margaret felt a sudden chill of apprehension course through her body. Nothing must happen to Robin. She couldn't bear it if it did.

"Let's take a walk after supper," Lord Ballender suggested. "It's a fine evening, meant to be enjoyed with pleasant company."

Margaret didn't like the idea of being seen with him, but her desire to get out and walk overrode her objections. "I would like that, yes," Margaret agreed, purposely keeping her feelings from showing. She longed to leave the castle walls. Here was her opportunity to do just that for a little while.

When they finished their meal, Gavin rose and reached for her arm. "Let's go for our stroll," he motioned, nodding toward the doorway.

They walked out through the arched doorway and moved into the circular tower leading upward to the battlements, Margaret making very sure she kept her distance. *It would be so easy to give in, to be overcome by his power!* But she knew it could only lead to a total lack of self-respect.

The memory of Lord Corleal should be a constant reminder of her proper place in relation to the man moving along at her side—as should the dark-haired beauty.

She and her companion reached the top step to the walk. A light brush of his hand along her waist caused Margaret to increase her pace and take her beyond his reach.

"It's a magnificent view from up here," he commented, indicating the unbroken expanse of sky and rolling emerald land spreading in all directions.

"Yes. The magnitude of God's handiwork makes one feel very small and insignificant. How wonderful to think that he is mindful of us at all."

"I admit that if I were ever tempted to believe in a Supreme Being, I'd believe from this height," Gavin conceded, studying the vastness of the land that dwarfed them.

Margaret turned aside to place her hands on the thick stone battlements and gaze into the waning light of evening. Her eyes swept to the burst of fire causing golden edges to line the dark clouds hovering in the west, all waiting for the silent drape of darkness to enfold them.

Gavin's eyes surveyed the landscape with pride. "Our land covers a thousand acres, much of it good dairy pasture." Leaning forward, his hands rested on the cold stone as he let his shoulder lightly brush against Margaret. "The castle and surrounding countryside have been in the Ballender family for three hundred years. The first Lord Ballender built this castle himself, as a stronghold against invasion."

Pointing to the arrow slits in the round towers—some long and straight, others in the form of a cross—he added, "The fortress has seen many battles with England over the last three hundred years. The difference in the color of stone shows where the armies battered the towers and curtain walls—battering that required periodic rebuilding. But the enemy never took the castle." His pride in his ancestors was obvious. Then pushing up with his hands he moved on across the castle walkway with Margaret moving along to accompany him.

"Now you allow an Englishwoman to sleep and eat and walk in your castle," she teasingly reminded the Scot. "Aren't you afraid?"

Lord Ballender let a slight flash of amusement—one that disappeared almost as abruptly as it appeared—play across his face as well. "If you think you will be rescued by force—such as an army from Corleal Castle—forget it. Lord Corleal's soldiers haven't a chance of getting through my gatehouse."

His words hurled her back to reality, a reality that reminded her of the lord of Corleal Castle and what he meant to her.

"You have no reason to keep me here!" she objected. Her gaze was set straight ahead, her hands tensing.

Gavin took Margaret's arm and turned her back toward the stairway. "I have my reasons." Force vibrated in his every word. The two cut across the barmkin and beyond the gatehouse to the fields surrounding the castle before he broke the silence once more.

"A messenger came today with a letter telling me that my uncle, Lord Carlton, is unwell. I must go to him as soon as possible." His words were clipped as he walked and explained the situation.

"Your uncle, milord?" Margaret's eyes were drawn to Gavin immediately, recalling the man who had ridden in and inquired about Master Campbell.

"Apparently you weren't told."

"No. But then, why would I?" she said.

"Well, no matter," answered Gavin, standing with hands clasped behind him, eyes squinting to the northeast to study the sky. "In fact, he wouldn't be calling for me at all if he had another heir to leave his estates to. But he hasn't."

"Surely that's not true, milord," retorted Margaret.

Lord Ballender began to pace. He took several steps beyond her then turned abruptly at her comment. "You think not?" His brows rose above his nose and his chin lifted.

"How could he feel that way?" she objected, curiously watching him as she challenged his thinking.

"Quite easily. We have never seen straight away on anything in our lives. We're both woven of the same stubborn fiber."

Margaret stared at the young man and watched him move impatiently about. "Where is your uncle?" she asked.

"In Edinburgh. I'm going there, anyway, with Robin, for we are to appear before the Regent shortly."

"What is to become of me?"

"You will go along, of course."

"No!" Margaret's cry was involuntary. "You've no right to do this to me!" She turned, sparks of defiance blazing in her eyes. "This morning you led me to believe that I'd return to England shortly. When I asked about my dresses you said I would need my wedding garments and I assumed—" Here her voice trailed away. The fresh ray of sunlit hope that he'd tossed out earlier was now a chunk of lead sinking in water.

Lord Ballender came up behind her and forced Margaret to face him. He drew her close to him and pressed his lips against hers. She struggled and attempted to jerk her head to one side, but his strength was too great. Then just as suddenly as he had grasped her to him, he eased his embrace and held her at arm's length.

"You misinterpreted my words. I didn't have Corleal in mind at all."

chapter
12

THE RETINUE GATHERED at daybreak in the barmkin of Ballender Castle and filed through the castle gate with Lord Ballender and eight soldiers in the lead. Robin followed. Margaret, perched upon a chestnut from the stables, and dressed in her riding garments, rode alongside. A hasty glance assured her that her Arabian was not among them. Four soldiers brought up the rear behind pack horses and servants.

A soft breeze blew from the southwest, twisting strands of golden hair around Margaret's face. Her skirt flapped lightly with the motion of the horse as she recalled embarking on her last trip, a short time ago, when her destination had been Corleal Castle. To her surprise, though the horror was still clear in her mind, she found that her pain was lessening, the picture fading. She was saddened to think that the memory of her father was now hazy and her life at Chilton Manor was fading. Even her mental visions of Lord Corleal were diminishing. At this point, she was no more sure of her future, or her destination, than she had been the first day of her capture. But one thing was certain: she was no longer a prisoner in Ballender Castle. For that, she was thankful.

Fresh air surrounded her now and a green landscape lay all around. And she was on a horse once again. Margaret sent a silent plea heavenward, for Lord Corleal's chances of finding her were diminishing at an alarming rate. *Go with me, Lord,* she breathed. *I don't know your eventual plan for my life, but whatever it is, help me to accept it.*

Margaret looked ahead at the men riding in single file over the long, arched sandstone bridge spanning the river. All wore helmets and leather doublets with swords at their sides and long spears pointing to the fore—emergency gear. Life was filled with emergencies and uncertainties in this bleak northern country. Lord Ballender's spirited stallion was already in the lead, ahead of the soldiers by three lengths. The nobleman rode straight in the saddle, broad-shouldered, not once turning to make sure his retinue followed closely behind him as ordered.

The golden tints of dawn streaked full-length across the blue of the sky with not a cloud to mar its expanse. A stirring of apprehension, as a morning breeze, crossed Margaret's face in anticipation of what lay ahead. No tree broke the full view of the sunrise from the line of travelers heading toward the rising hazy glow of sun on the horizon. The meadows were tinged with white and pale pink drifts of cow-parsley, and angelica sparkled with droplets of diamond wetness from earlier showers. Here the world was at peace; it seemed a sacrilege to disturb the hallowed silence.

With Robin riding by her side, Margaret knew that wherever she went, or whatever happened to her, Robin would be her mainstay to see that no harm came to her. He was a calming force. She was thankful that God supplied someone like the tailor to encourage her heart and her faith. Margaret longed to ask him about his travels and his preaching, but no one broke the stillness surrounding them. There would be plenty of time on this journey to question Robin about his ministry.

When the procession veered to the left and followed along a rough northerly roadway, Robin was first to speak. "As we wend our way north, Margaret, we will join with other nobles and gentlemen and preachers from the western and southern parts of Scotland traveling to Edinburgh. We don't know what will happen when we stand before the Regent, but we do know that it's impossible to allow the French to pour into our country in such great numbers and threaten our freedom."

"Will there be a battle?"

"In all likelihood, yes. I'm afraid it can't be avoided. The anger and hatred of injustices runs too deep to turn back the hurt. The Bishop of St. Andrews made an attempt at smoothing things over, but it was a failure."

"But are the Regent and the French soldiers well armed?"

"Yes. Unfortunately the Regent has been fortifying herself with French troops for some time, using our Scottish forts as her garrisons. We have no mighty nobles to back us, nor organized armies, but that doesn't matter. God will provide," he added, assurance ringing through his words. "He is with us, Margaret. When Gideon had too many men, God ordered him to send most of them home so they couldn't win by strength alone. God is all-powerful."

She hoped fervently that Robin was right. The French possessed a well-trained army; Scotland did not. But she knew God could help in a hopeless situation such as this. Had he not done it for the people throughout the centuries who had turned to him in their helplessness and desperation? And he would do it again.

Unconsciously, Margaret's eyes shifted back to the darkly handsome Lord Ballender leading the procession. She refused to admit that her heart betrayed her when she compared him with Lord Corleal, for between the two, she could see no similarities. But of one thing Margaret was sure—she would not go back on her vow to Lord Corleal, regardless of the cost.

By late afternoon, the village of Ballender was left far behind and the high barren moors, dwarfing the travelers with their rounded, weathered peaks, surrounded them. When a massive stone castle, perched atop a hazy summit, came into view, Lord Ballender urged his stallion toward that mark.

Black-faced sheep milled about, nibbling the emerald growth on the steep sides of the wind-swept hills. Over the next rise, the village hugged the summit beneath the walled fortress. Each stone house rested in its protective shelter of the fortress, clinging like a calf to its mother.

"We'll rest here tonight and get an early start in the morning," explained Robin. "The lord of these lands will accompany us to Edinburgh to join us when we meet with the Regent as she has demanded."

The procession skirted the hill, wending its way up the rise to the village before proceeding on to the castle gatehouse. All the aches and discomforts of her former journey came back to Margaret, and with them, a suspicion, a leery reaction to the very sight of the castle and to thoughts of their destination in Edinburgh.

"This fortress is not as large as Ballender Castle," Robin explained, "but it is older. It was built as protection against the northern clans of Scots, who would swoop down from their wild, craggy haunts to capture cattle and take grain from the lowland farmers back to their encampments."

"Your countrymen are not noted for their placidness."

"I fear not," he agreed with a smile.

Margaret was shown to a small room built within the thickness of the castle wall and was given water for washing the grime of the journey from her face and hands. After changing into the better of her two plain gowns, she made herself as decent as she could before joining the others for supper. The question of why she was given a castle chamber to sleep in rather than a pile of heather in the servants' hall occurred to her, but she accepted her accomodations with a thankful heart.

Lord Auchler was a large, burly man possessed of curly hair and beard, a wide forehead, and pale eyes that exuded kindness. If he questioned her presence among his guests, he gave no outward indication. Lord Ballender must have provided an adequate excuse for her being with the Ballender party.

The great vaulted hall, freshly whitewashed up to the oak ceiling beam, was furnished with monstrous oak tables, placed in the shape of a U. White linen cloths covered all of them.

Servants carried in joints of mutton and lamb plus silver platters piled high with herring and bread and fruit for the guests' supper. Each servant stood quietly by awaiting the signal to serve. The seating plan had Margaret and Robin side-by-side, necessitating conversation only with him. For that she was grateful. But they remained near enough their host to hear his words.

"What answers has John Knox sent from Geneva? Will he come back anytime soon to lead us?"

Lord Ballender shook his head, simultaneously stabbing a large chunk of mutton. "He said he wouldn't return until the country is ready. From what I can see, we are more than ready to throw off these cursed French. He can come back immediately." With this, he consumed a huge bite of the meat.

"Aye, Gavin, but it takes full dedication for Reform," objected Lord Auchler with a shake of his head. "I'm not so sure that all our nobles are ready to completely count the cost of such a move. It will take a great amount of money to fight against France."

"What more incentive do we need to convince them?" exploded the younger man. "The life is being choked out of us. We're being overrun and overpowered by these foreigners."

"Of that, all of us are convinced, yes," answered Lord Auchler calmly, "but not everyone has our will to succeed. Until that goal is achieved, we will do well to bide our time in waiting for full backing and the ability to move forward with force.

"More and more of the nobility, ignored by the Regent, are joining our cause. And we have God on our side. He works in mysterious ways to help his people and he may yet send a willing England to give us the help we desperately need."

"There's little joy in that," objected Gavin. "They would just as soon ignore us. But we have one advantage: if we are conquered by France, England will be next in line for the same fate. The French will stop at nothing once they get that sweet taste of victory in their mouths. England will take none of France's nonsense."

Margaret studied Lord Ballender in the lantern light. His features were animated, his eyes bright with the thrill of challenge. Not once did she perceive, in the faces of the three men gathered at the table, the faintest flicker of emotion other than immutable loyalty to their cause. Robin and Lord Auchler placed their faith in God; Lord

Ballender, in England. In time perhaps he, too, would place his faith in the Supreme Being. *But that will take a miracle.*

Margaret lay in her bed that night, staring into the blackness of the room. What was her role in all this? And what did Lord Ballender want of her? Why was he going to all the trouble of taking her to Edinburgh when there seemed to be no purpose in it? Wouldn't it have been simpler just to send her back to Corleal and be done with her? So many questions; so few answers.

The following day the skies turned a stone gray and a light rain fell as the string of horsemen made its way slowly from the southwesterly direction and entered through the old and failing West Port Gate of Edinburgh. For a few moments Lord Ballender and Lord Auchler spoke quietly together before parting. Then nodding, the younger man headed his stallion up a steep wynd leading to the cobbled main street of Edinburgh—High Street. The animals' hoofs on the square stones of pavement clattered in an uneven rhythm to accompany the bustle of activity: housewives with market baskets swinging from their arms, the clamor of tradesmen, fishwomen, and children at work and play in the background.

Margaret hastily glanced about her at the lines of stone houses bordering both sides of the street. Years of smoke and soot from stone chimneys had blackened the outside façades. Each dwelling was at least two or three stories high, one tightly hugging the next, with windows facing the busy main street. All the houses were topped with steep slants of thatch, made from neat, thick layers of oat straw and heather to repel the elements.

Within the ground floor of each house was the kitchen. In booths constructed along the front of each were business establishments bordering the main street of the town. Outside stone steps led up to the living quarters of the businessmen, or burgesses, in the second and upper stories of the houses. Here and there small dark closes led the way into courtyards enclosed by other stone buildings, their stones also blackened from the smoke of many chimneys.

The party turned onto an intersecting wynd, and followed it to its end. The mansion, the last stone dwelling, featured a high wall, running parallel with the house and ending abruptly on the slope to the North Loch below. The house was one of the few that sat on its own parcel of ground, with gardens and orchards to the rear and sides. A malt barn and cow-bil were to the rear of Lord Carlton's estate.

Lord Ballender slipped from his stallion and disappeared inside the house while the soldiers and servants rode on to stable the horses. After preliminary arrangements were attended to, the party from Ballender waited outside for further instructions.

Margaret strolled over to the plum orchard and stared up into the pleasant foliage. Robin followed with the aid of his crutch. "What is to become of us?" she asked him.

"We'll stay here awhile and take our lives one day at a time. As you know, we don't face times of peace."

"I saw hundreds of soldiers as we rode through the town."

"Yes. Edinburgh is overrun with them, and what I have heard about French soldiers is not good. Don't go from the house unaccompanied. These Frenchmen have neither respect nor courtesy for our Scottish women, and I doubt seriously if they have any for their own women."

Gavin came from the house and met Margaret and Robin with a scowl as black as tar. "Doddering old fool," he muttered. "He refuses to listen to reason—as usual."

"Come," said Robin. "Have patience with him—he is old."

"They told me he was ill. Ha! He's in better health than I. But, enough of that. Come. I will show you to your rooms." Gavin turned and ran lightly up the steps once more. "It seems he has sent most of the servants packing. No doubt they couldn't tolerate his vile tongue any longer. Little wonder!"

"He has no one to care for him at all?" asked Margaret, a look of shock washing over her face.

"His old servant, William, and the cook stayed. It's good that I brought a few servants along. We'll put them into service and use the soldiers to fill in."

"Don't be too sure," warned Robin. "The soldiers won't take to that too well."

"Rubbish. They'll do it if they want to earn their pay!" he growled.

So, thought Margaret, *when he said he and his uncle were cut of the same stubborn fiber, he spoke no lie.*

The mansion was built of fine, smooth ashlar stone and was set apart from other houses by high stone walls. It rose, crowstepped and multichimneyed, several stories into the air amidst the orchards and gardens surrounding it. Those same trees partially hid the barn and cow-bil from view.

Gavin led the way up one side of the divided and symmetrically shaped front forestairs to the entrance. Above the door lintel rested an imbedded stone panel with the inscription, "God Be Merciful," carved in bold, stand-out letters. Margaret smiled at the sight of it there. With both Gavin and his uncle in the same house, she mused, they certainly needed all the storehouse of mercy God could provide.

"I'll introduce you later," Gavin told Margaret. "When he's human, that is. For now, see what you can do about whipping the servants into orderly service."

chapter

13

MARGARET'S NEW POSITION OF AUTHORITY gave her a much-needed reason to take an interest in her surroundings. She sought help from William, the old man's serving man, but his overwhelming duty to the elder Lord Carlton's constant demands prohibited his spending much time with her in guiding her to her own duties.

A conversation with Sophia, the cook, proved more beneficial. Satisfied she was fulfilling her obligations, she decided to survey the domain and moved to the Great Hall.

There she discovered the old man sitting before the fire. She stopped abruptly at the sight of him, undecided whether to beg his pardon, and leave, or to speak. He, in turn, surveyed her thoroughly before he opened his mouth to speak.

"Who are you?" he demanded, letting his gaze come to rest on her hair. Margaret recalled a similar comment from his nephew on their first meeting behind the castle. Her temptation to smile was quelled, however, by the anger spreading across a face that was an aging replica of his nephew's.

"Milord, I—" But before she could get the words out of her mouth, he interrupted discourteously, an obvious amount of open disgust lining his face.

"You are one of Gavin's mistresses, aren't you? The young whelp!" His voice rose in intensity like thunder. "I'll not have it. That slut from Ballender, Elizabeth Stanus, called Betty—the wine merchant's daughter, she is—thinks she'll get her greedy hands on both my nephew and my lands. Ha! I'll not leave him one coin until he marries a lady. You're wasting your time if you think you will fare better!" With a grim look on his face that spoke of pure rage, he gave his cane one powerful whack on the floor as added reinforcement to his invective and ground his teeth in a torrid, indignant display of fury.

Boiling indignation rippled through Margaret's body. *So, the reivers brought me to Ballender so their leader wouldn't lose his inheritance!* She bristled from deep within.

If Lord Gavin Ballender thought she would consent to this plan, he had a big surprise in store. Her betrothal to Lord Corleal was still valid, and Lord Corleal's bethrothed she would remain! Margaret turned, too furious to deny Lord Carlton's charges, and marched out of the room. But deep inside, the tiny seed of hurt that sprouted there overshadowed even her raging burst of anger.

The day of the summons to the Regent's palace—July twentieth—was gloomy and rainy, but the weather conditions failed to deter the stalwart intent of the gathering Scottish preachers and lords. They were to complete their mission—to appear before the Regent to answer for their behavior. They resolved to march before her, their heads held high.

Robin and Gavin rose early to breakfast with Margaret. Robin insisted they join hands to petition God's help in the coming meeting, so he stretched out his arms to each of them.

Dear Robin, Margaret thought as he prayed aloud, *how perfectly fine you are. What a simple faith is yours, running so deep and unblemished.* Her fingers clasped Gavin's and Robin's and though she determined not to let Lord Ballender's touch affect her, she found her pulse throbbing at a faster rate. His hand was warm on hers, the pressure firm, with a slight pulsating rhythm in the contact that matched her own.

Gavin and Robin left the house to meet fellow Scotsmen at the Mercat Cross on High Street, with Margaret's fervent wishes for their well-being. The anguish of their hearts spilled onto the fertile soil of her own and she felt the maturing sprouts of hurt for them. But what would happen when Gavin's boiling temper faced an equally determined enemy—the Regent—at her palatial residence, Holyrood House, at the lower end of High Street?

Margaret had determined, in Gavin's absence, to avoid any further contact with his uncle. His accusations—directed at his nephew, and at herself—still burned in her ears. Another encounter could prove only as unpleasant, she knew. But how long could she hide from Lord Carlton?

Two days—for that length of time she managed to bypass him by involving herself in righting the house, which had deteriorated to a deplorable state, to impeccable order. She refolded linens in the evenings while Robin told her of the day's events.

"Was there fighting?" Margaret inquired with mounting interest.

"None, other than words. The Regent sat with her boldfaced lieges—their gazes calculating and cold—behind her. Our men spoke plainly and focused the blame for our troubles squarely on her counselors, accusing them of oppression and murder. She was full of sweetness, pretending to have no knowledge of our trouble. Some were fooled into believing her; others saw through the fickle speech immediately."

"And Lord Ballender?"

"He exploded, of course. It's his opinion she can't be trusted any farther than he can throw his horse."

"And is it yours, too, Robin?"

"Yes. But time will tell."

When the Regent, a few days later, demanded that the Scotsmen make public apology on St. Giles Day for their June burning of the statue, Gavin exploded. "So much for her great sincerity toward our grievances! I would like to take some of our stupidly gullible men and rub their noses in that sincerity!

As Margaret knew it must, her success in hiding from Lord Carlton came to an end. But her much-dreaded encounter proved to be of little ado. With notable suddenness, the old man's attitude toward her changed completely. He was actually quite civil to her, if a bit condescending, calling at times for her to come to him and bring wine or a pillow or the menu for the day.

Though she had not been able to bring herself to discuss his accusations with his nephew, because of their nature, she realized from the happenings that Gavin must have heard about the incident and set matters straight about her presence in the house.

Margaret prayed for guidance in dealing with the elder man. She came to the conclusion that remaining servile, while polite, was her best tack, and his attitude toward her continued to improve, to the point he depended on her to run his house in the efficient manner she had displayed. He became almost a friend, though she was careful to never let down the bounds of her station as housekeeper. He was still the lord; she, a captive.

In August he asked Margaret to accompany him in a turn about the orchard. "My plums are nearly ripe, so I watch them daily. A quick frost could kill them all in a few moments' time. They are my favorites, these plums, and I'd be furious if they were ruined right under my nose. This cold northern climate is unpredictable, to say the least." He inspected the fruit and turned suddenly toward the young woman beside him.

"Tell me, what is that nephew of mine up to these days? He spends a great amount of time with the young tailor, who, I'm told, has also become a preacher. I like Robin but I suspect my nephew and he are keeping company with those rebels who plot against the Regent."

"I know little, milord, except that the poor people suffer untold misery from the burial and marriage fees forced upon them by the Regent. From my understanding, French soldiers are pouring into the country in great numbers." Margaret realized that she was beginning to understand the Scottish Reformers' anguish and develop a deep feeling for their unbearable plight.

"They went with this rebellious group to the Regent's chambers not long ago?"

"So I was told."

"The fools. They'll get us involved in a war with France, and we'll be blown into the North Sea. What can be accomplished by their going about Scotland stirring up controversy and hoping to win enough support to fight against the well-regulated French army and the powerful clergy? It's utter madness!"

Margaret sat silently. Her mind told her the old man was right—the French were more likely to keep the control unless God undertook for the Reformers—but somewhere, in her heart, she took her stand with Robin.

The old man continued to regard her, and when he again spoke, it was not a complaint against his nephew, but an expression of concern for her well-being. "I believe we have gowns stored in the trunks to fit you. That plain, coarse dress you wear is not proper for a lady."

"What I have is comfortable, milord. Please don't bother."

"Nonsense. I'll have William find them and bring them to the Hall."

The gowns William brought from the trunks that evening were, on command of Lord Carlton, tried for size and fitted before Margaret appeared before him to model them as ordered.

"These dresses are fit for the Regent, herself," said Sophia, the cook, who in the absence of another woman, had been enlisted to help Margaret dress. "Lady Ballender wore them to the palace in the grand days when our Regent's husband, King James, was alive and ruled Scotland. Those were happy times for milady." She ran her fingers over the rich velvets and silks bordered with gold bouillon or pearl—or both.

"Milord has not ordered them brought out since her death, so it's a special honor, you see, for him to allow you to wear them. She was your size," the cook commented, making a comparison, letting her eyes run the full length of Margaret's frame. "You'll look bonny in these gowns with your light hair. Hers was black as pitch."

Margaret slipped into the ebony velvet and felt the slim bodice, the puffed upper sleeves tapering to the wrist. She eyed the flow of the sweeping skirt. "It's lovely," whispered Margaret, "but it's a waste. Where would I ever wear them?"

Sophia sighed. "I can't say. Times are not happy as they once were." She gave a sad shake of her head in response to her own statement. The cook fussed and clucked over Margaret, arranging her gown dutifully before assessing her handiwork. Standing off to a side and critically eyeing her efforts, the cook gave her one final piece of advice. "Go on down. Milord is in for one great surprise!"

Dutifully Margaret made her way down the stairs toward the Hall. Instead of dreaming of Lord Corleal and his reaction if he were to see her in the costly gown—as she should have, Margaret knew—her thoughts swerved to Gavin Ballender. She quickly bit her lip and silently rebuked herself for her folly. To him she was no more than the means to saving his inheritance. And to that end, she'd never submit.

Instead of finding the old man sitting hunched over his cane alone, as usual, Margaret saw four men directing curious glances in her direction. The light from the fire cast soft shadows upon the velvet gown and pale flowing hair, drawing gasps of pleasure at first glimpse of her. Margaret's face flushed crimson. She would have fled but for the old man's bellow, "Margaret! Come here!"

The idea of being ogled like a new painting or a decorated dish was distasteful to her, but her station dictated that she obey his orders. Her eyes were purposely riveted to the old man to keep them from wandering foolishly to his nephew.

"Come here," he repeated, this time almost gently. "Lady Carlton wore that gown when King James married his first French princess." He sighed deeply and stared at the beautiful girl standing before him. "Those were marvelous days, my dear. Long gone."

Margaret knew that Lord Ballender, also, intensely scrutinized her, but she chose not to notice, keeping her eyes strictly on his uncle. Her mind required even stricter discipline.

"Sit down beside me," the old man instructed, "while we visit together."

Margaret acquiesced. She folded her hands uneasily in her lap and forced her thoughts to absorb the news that was being shared before her entrance into the room caused the interruption.

Lord Auchler raised his glass to his lips and broke the silence of the moment. "The town burgesses were commanded by the bishops to resurrect the St. Giles image that was burned in June or pay to have a new one made for the St. Giles Day parade here in Edinburgh."

"Of course," burst in Lord Carlton, his voice rising in irritation. "Why shouldn't they? It was plain vandalism to rid the church of its patron saint."

"Nonsense," countered Gavin, his temper accelerating in defense. "Why should the church tell us what we may or may not do? These are public funds and, as such, have no business being used for the church."

"The town's people had no right to destroy church property!" stormed Lord Carlton in swift response.

Robin spoke quietly to the old man. "The Scriptures speak out strongly against any form of idolatry, milord, and this statue was the French patron saint and worshiped as such. The people are groaning under French oppression. In destroying the statue, the people substituted their frustration against an image that stood for oppression against them."

"A harmless image standing in the church? Ridiculous! It's been there for years. This was just an excuse for the rabble to loot and destroy. Let the town pay for that act!" the old man bellowed. Thus spoken, he rose and stormed out of the room to go to his chamber. "Fools. All of you! William! Where are you?"

"Hopeless old dolt," spat Gavin impatiently. "The bishop told his curate to curse the chief magistrate black as coal for not consenting to use public money to buy a new image. The magistrate dared the bishop to find a lawful warrant. But the bishop couldn't find one. What will my uncle say when these French soldiers take over his house before long?"

"They may not," pointed out Lord Auchler. "He's not against the Regent."

Robin excused himself to retire to his room, limping a little more than usual. Lord Auchler rose, likewise, and took his leave.

"Black velvet certainly becomes you with your golden hair," Gavin told Margaret, his eyes mirroring the appreciation within his heart.

"Thank you, milord."

"Let's walk in the garden," he suggested, rising. "The moon shining on the North Loch is brilliant and full tonight, and I want you to view it with me."

What choice did she have? He'd not take no for an answer and would take hold of her arm to make sure she accompanied him in his walk. Margaret walked through the plum orchard, Gavin by her side, but she kept a safe distance between them.

The earlier rain had ceased and the moon now made long silvery paths across the ripples from one side of the loch to the other. From where she stood, Margaret observed a branch from one of the plum trees cascading across the white surface of the moon. A soft movement of air whispered through the foliage overhead. With the stirring came an involuntary shudder passing through Margaret's body and she realized how foolish she was to remain in the man's company. She turned to retrace her steps back to the house.

"Where are you going?" Gavin asked. His hands closed immediately around her shoulders.

"I'm returning to the house, for I'm getting cold."

"I have a simple remedy for that," he whispered, letting his lips graze her neck.

"No doubt," Margaret admitted, pulling away. "But you have no right to take liberties, for I am a betrothed woman. That fact hasn't changed simply because I'm no longer in Ballender."

Gavin's response was curt. "And I prefer to forget."

chapter
14

WHEN THE COOK informed Margaret of her need for more spices, Margaret immediately seized on the opportunity to walk to the High Street market herself and purchase the necessary condiments. Since she was no longer a prisoner, and Lord Ballender was too immersed in the political problems of the country to worry himself about her, she relished her newfound freedom to come and go as she pleased.

"Are the markets open today?" Margaret asked Sophia.

"Yes. But most of the buying is done in the morning."

Remembering the warning about the French soldiers in town, Margaret decided to ask Robin to go with her. He spent part of each day making new doublets, breeches, and hose for Lord Carlton so he wouldn't be a debtor while staying in the old man's house. But Margaret was sure Robin could spare an hour for a little exercise.

At breakfast, Gavin broke his silence of deep concentration with a sudden piece of information. "My uncle made one of his rare comments of appreciation yesterday." Lord Ballender shoved a piece of toasted bread into his mouth. Glancing at Margaret's puzzled expression, he added, "He tells me that since you have been here, the house is becoming a home once again—it's clean, pleasant and bustling with activity."

A sparkle appeared in the ebony depths of Gavin's eyes as he observed the slight flush of his breakfast partner. He reached over and covered Margaret's hand with his own. "I agree with him, Margaret. You have a way of brightening a place even without smiling. But I'm convinced the smiles will come in time."

Margaret answered nothing. Though the words appeared heartfelt, she suspected his intentions centered around one goal in life: his inheritance. How far, she wondered, would he go to achieve that goal? With a slight show of intended indifference, she said, "It's my job, milord. And it keeps my mind off—"

"Off?" he questioned. A contemplative look buried itself in Margaret's blue eyes.

She bit her lip in embarrassment, for she had almost blurted out, "off you," catching herself in time to avoid that blunder. Instead, she qualified her remark with, "off the problems at hand."

"Oh?" He shot a sideways glance at Margaret, then chuckled. "Since we seem to be meant to spend time together, could you not begin to call me Gavin?"

"I could not do so, milord. I am but a servant in your uncle's house. In that capacity, I will go to High Street market this morning for spices."

"Not alone," he bristled with stiff objection.

"No, not alone. I'll ask Robin to go with me."

"Fine," Gavin conceded, "but don't ever go alone. It isn't safe in this town anymore." The comment prompted a bitterness that spread across his face as a black scowl. He rose and warned her again. "Be careful, won't you, Margaret? I don't want to lose you."

"Yes, of course." She felt a vain desire surfacing—a longing that Lord Ballender—Gavin—might perhaps feel a genuine interest toward her for herself alone, without the underlying need to rescue his tottering inheritance. But she rebuked such a thought as soon as it registered in her brain. *Lord,* she pleaded from her heart, *strengthen me. I must never give in to such urges.*

After Gavin left and Lord Carlton had eaten breakfast Margaret asked him a question. "I am going to High Street. Can I bring you something to read?"

114

"Why would you? I couldn't read it."

"I could read to you."

With shock registering in his aging face, the old man turned his gaze toward his new housekeeper. "You can read and write?"

"Yes," Margaret smiled with an accompanying nod of her head.

"Good. Choose anything you like and I'll listen." He allowed a rare touch of amusement to crease the face that was not used to such exercise, nor to such kindness.

"I will," she promised. Unconsciously, Margaret patted his arm with affection before turning away. She was happier than she'd been since she was brought so unwillingly to this country, for she had a new—though reluctant—friend in Lord Carlton. Perhaps he filled the void in her life for the father she no longer had.

The wind was brisk, swirling from the southwest in waves of late summer freshness over a thickly populated town reeking of many odors—some pleasant, some foul and disagreeable. Shops lined both sides of the street. Margaret walked beside Robin and took note of booksellers, upholsterers, tailors, cloth shops, bake shops, fish markets, gold and silver merchants. A huge stone church caught her interest for it extended out into High Street and reached high above the thoroughfare on the right. Could that impressive edifice possibly be the St. Giles cathedral, the scene of the seizing of the statue and subsequent burning in June? A simple questioning of Robin proved her theory was correct.

As Robin and Margaret followed the main street, they were aware of a gathering at the Mercat Cross a short way beyond the church. Out of curiosity, they drew near to the assembled crowd to listen.

Margaret watched a drummer beat vigorously to draw attention to a man, parchment in his hand, climbing the worn stone steps leading up to an overhead platform atop the Mercat Cross. He began in a booming monotone, "We declare ourselves enemies to, and forsake the foreign faith—the faith of Satan—" Margaret moved closer to Robin and stared at the man who dared openly stand and give such an announcement in the very town where the

Regent and her counselors resided. After the whole proclamation was read, they heard the names of the men who had boldly put their signatures to the manifesto.

"What will happen now?" Margaret whispered. "Are the signers really in danger of their lives?" Her mind swiftly turned to Gavin and his dauntless ways, his determination to see justice done in Scotland. Did he really understand the full depth of what he was doing or was it just an exciting new game of chance—a fresh rally to put his boundless energies behind? Lord Ballender made no pretense about his disinterest in the desire for a true faith in God. His was simply an anger against the mushrooming French domination of his country. To Gavin, weapons alone were the answer to his country's problems.

As soon as the herald finished, Margaret heard the citizens give full vent to their feelings. They decried the French soldiers—guilty of every form of excess imaginable—and the uncaring Regent and her churchmen. The townsmen's anger rose in savage uproar.

With a deep sigh, Robin leaned heavily on his crutch and walked alongside Margaret as they wended their way toward the Upper Bow Street to get spices. Passing by a couple of French soldiers, Robin and Margaret heard them call out filthy comments from their casually leaning positions against the stone wall of a close. Margaret's lips tightened. She clung to Robin, her face scarlet with embarrassment.

The day of the St. Giles parade was cold and clear. The southwest winds blew penetrating gusts, stirring the leaves of the plum trees and the ripening fruit.

"Margaret," insisted Lord Carlton, "come with me. Let's take a walk out to my orchard before the parade. I would like to see the entire spectacle, but I can't endure the standing anymore. Will you go?"

"Yes, I'll go." She was aware that the Reformers were commanded by the Regent to give a public apology because of the June burning of the image—the patron saint of the French. Robin had told her of his eagerness—along with that of all the city—to see what would happen. Margaret didn't relay this information to the old man, or her reasons for attending the parade. He'd find out soon enough.

"The town council didn't get the money for a new statue of St. Giles." Lord Carlton spat out his fury. "These Reformers—or Brethren—or whatever fool thing they call themselves, should have been made to pay for a new one! Such lawlessness. Why don't they let the government alone?"

"Your plums are ripening fast, milord," Margaret inserted hastily to change the subject, "I shall pick some for you." Immediately, she began plucking the ripe fruit and making a basket of her apron.

"Um. Just make sure they are good and ripe," he warned. As she reached up into the tree, both she and Lord Carlton saw Gavin racing from the cow-bil on his black stallion and hastily turn his mount toward High Street.

"Is the young fool going to honor St. Giles after all?" he asked, watching his nephew dash off, "or is he going to cause trouble? He'll come to no good if he keeps on this way."

Returning to the house in a disgruntled mood, he ordered the cook to make him plum tarts and then settled by the fire once more to doze and, perhaps, to think of bygone days of youth and peace.

Robin accompanied Margaret to High Street. A current of restlessness flowed through the assembled crowd. Many, mostly French, came to honor the patron saint; others came to see if the Scots would actually show humility by making a public apology at the Mercat Cross—as the Regent had demanded—for the June burning of the statue.

Within moments, every eye turned toward Edinburgh Castle, at the elevated west end of High Street. Drums rolled. Trumpets tore apart the morning air with their shrill blasts. The whining of the bagpipes preceded the royal, priestly banners fluttering in the breeze, and to the rear a magnificent coach was pulled along by six plumed horses.

"The Regent?" whispered Margaret.

"Aye. Her daughter was married in April to the son of the French king, as I mentioned before."

Yes, thought Margaret, *an arranged wedding such as mine. But the Princess Mary wasn't captured by a wild band of reivers on the way to her wedding ceremony as I was.*

Margaret watched the Regent sitting tall and straight in her carriage with the solemnity of the occasion imbued upon her face. The woman looked neither to the right nor to the left as she passed by the assemblage lining both sides of the street. Her officials followed with an alternate statue, nailed to a board, to replace the one the Scots had burned. All along the route, Margaret observed those in the crowd who bowed in homage to the image of St. Giles as it passed by them.

The parade proceeded slowly down the street from the castle, past St. Giles Church and the Mercat Cross. It moved steadily past rows of stone houses and shops to the towering Canongate. From here the parade angled through the gate to the Canongate Mercat Cross beyond. It turned about and returned again. The Regent ordered the carriage to stop at the home of Burgess Carpenter where she had planned to eat the feast of celebration to the patron saint. With much pomp she exited the coach and walked to the burgess's doorway.

Tension mounted to fever pitch. Suddenly the Reformers shouted a signal to attack. A familiar woman—the wine merchant's daughter—yelled and flayed her arms along with Gavin.

"Down with the idol!" they screamed. The mob roared in unison, "Down with the idol! Down with the idol!"

Margaret watched as the men raced onto the street, Gavin leading one of the groups, to grab the statue, hoist it into the air, and throw it to the stone pavement, breaking off the head. They took the remaining part and tossed it into the drainage ditch along the road—the common sewer. The yelling was deafening. But foremost in Margaret's whirling mind was the dark-haired woman at Gavin's side, cheering him on. Had she followed him to Edinburgh or had he invited her?

118

Margaret was jostled and pushed, roughly pitched from side to side. She vaguely felt Robin's firm fingers on her arm, pulling her clear of the wild, jubilant crowd before she was trampled to death in the push. Her thoughts raced back to the early days, since coming to Edinburgh, when Gavin had left the house and returned in the early hours of morning. Perhaps he was truly as immoral as his uncle painted him. Margaret knew she had no right to experience the pain that now pricked her heart. Gavin could never mean anything to her. His attentions toward her meant he was forced to marry a lady of genteel breeding in order to inherit his uncle's estates. His attempts to win her were an obvious sham. Both she and Gavin were forced into obligatory marriages. But she'd never submit to his advances. Never.

When the screams of the crowd brought Margaret back to reality, she witnessed the hasty flight of the Regent's lieges—men who had taken part in the parade but were now running for their lives from the angry mob.

"For now," Robin commented above the din, looking at the sea of faces around them, "the people's frustrations are given a temporary release from the hopelessness of their situation. The smashing of that idol represented the ridding of the Scottish shore of its French burden and accompanying abuses. But soon these same people will pay the supreme sacrifice for the cause of freedom—their lives."

Margaret gave Robin a quick, anxious glance. "It's frightening," she breathed, her voice taut.

"Freedom has a price. It always does."

Margaret refused to turn to see what had happened to Gavin and Betty Stanus. She supposed they vanished into the crowd. Silently, Margaret walked alongside Robin as they again made their way down High Street.

Is this woman one Gavin truly admires? Does he long to have her by his side for the rest of his life? Would he give up his inheritance for her? Surely Lord Carlton would not . . .

Margaret thought of the fire of opposition blazing between

Gavin and his uncle. *Yes, I think he would disinherit him, at that,* she concluded. Then straightening, she again sent up a plea for help in pushing the dashing figure, the dazzling smile, the sparkling eyes from her mind.

Will Lord Corleal ever find me here? A long weary sigh escaped her lips.

chapter
15

SHORTLY AFTER SUPPER, Gavin came into the rushlit kitchen as Margaret carried his uncle's tray and dishes to a large pan to be washed. Despite her stern resolve to remain unaffected by him, she felt her heartbeat involuntarily increase. With a voice that carefully masked the emotional depths within her, Margaret asked, "Have you had supper?"

"No," he answered, darting a devastating wink her way. "But you can prepare some for me."

Margaret immediately took a sharp knife and sliced a thick portion of beef for his evening meal. Then, reaching into a dish for a plum tart, she placed his food on a small platter and put it in front of him.

"Did you go to the parade?" he questioned absently.

"Yes." Turning, she noticed the cook was finished with the dishes and was looking around to see if any others were lying about.

"Sophia, you can leave. I'll finish up." Margaret advised her. The woman gave her a grateful nod.

"You managed that smoothly," Gavin commented with a chuckle after the cook left.

"The woman is tired," she explained quietly, realizing the import of his words, and aiming to dispel the possibility of any ulterior motives on her part.

"Sit down with me," he invited, pointing to the chair next to his.

"It's been an exciting day. No doubt we'll hear from the Regent about today's actions soon enough, but our retaliation today gave everyone plenty of satisfaction in venting our anger and frustration. Before the end of this, the Regent and her cohorts are going to know our intentions are deadly serious."

Robin came down the steps with his sewing in hand, moving quietly to the table where Margaret and Gavin sat in the stillness of the rushlight. In his arms he carried the Bible.

"Will you take time to help us with our reading and writing, once more?" he asked, aiming his request at Margaret.

"Yes." She took Gavin's dishes and washed them while the two men discussed the day's happenings. Then she returned to the table to begin her work.

After an hour, Robin stretched and slowly closed his Bible. His comments were directed toward Gavin when he looked up again. "You know, don't you, that John Willock is very sick?"

"I have heard, yes." Gavin leaned back in his chair and casually stretched his legs full length in front of him as he gave full attention to Robin's words.

"Even though he's ill, he continues to preach from his bed." The tailor folded his arms in front of him and leaned on the table to continue his comments. "I've never heard a man with more wisdom and good common sense. He had some excellent suggestions about public reform in his discussions with the lords and the town provost. When he spoke, I felt like the beggar sitting at the rich man's table." Robin folded his hands beneath his mouth in contemplation. "Why," he asked, looking directly at Gavin, "doesn't Willock go to the Regent and talk to her? Surely he could get her to listen to reason if anyone could."

"It would do no good," countered Lord Ballender, obvious ire intertwining his words. "She's stiff-necked as a cock fighting a dog. What we need to do is gather an army of leading men of the country and march in and get this business over quickly—before she has time to know what has hit her." Gavin's eyes narrowed as he delivered his remedy for the Regent and her stubbornness.

"That would take ships and supplies and cannon. Let's pray our plight doesn't reach that point," Robin implored, "for the poor would be hardest hit of all. Their crops would be destroyed, their men killed. They can't afford those added miseries." He paused. "I still think that if someone could convince the Regent—"

Gavin cut in impatiently. "You know as well as I do, Robin, such an idea is futile. Have you forgotten what she did after we met with her at her palace? Eh?" He sat upright, his eyes blazing with full recollection of that unfortunate meeting at the palace. "The lords talked today, for some time, about a peaceful Reformation. Some have written to John Knox urging him to return as soon as possible." Gavin drew a deep breath, and expelled it with the statement, "All I can say is he'd better come soon."

"I agree," Robin said, conceding on points discussed. "But we must try all peaceful means first. Then, if that fails, we will at least know we explored every alternative before taking up arms."

Robin rose and excused himself so he could go to bed. Margaret seized on the opportunity to do the same. She started to rise, but Gavin placed his hand on her arm.

"Don't go yet," he insisted.

She settled herself in the chair next to him as requested but sat on the edge of her seat to let him know she didn't intend staying long in his company.

"You are a pleasure to come home to," he pointed out, his dark glittering eyes flashing the approval from deep within.

"Don't become accustomed to my being here," Margaret warned quietly, knowing as she said the words that they were unconvincing—to herself as well.

A long, drawn-out sigh passed over his lips. He placed his hand on her shoulder, letting his fingers knead the back of her neck. "Still waiting, aren't you?" he responded tightly. "You still haven't given up hope of Corleal's finding you."

"No, milord, I haven't." Then with a slight rise to her chin she added, "He'll find me one day; of that, I have no doubt."

"Do you really want him to, Margaret?"

She didn't want to answer that statement, deciding that it was time she left this conversation, for it was causing her to tremble slightly within. His hand on her neck warned her of her feelings toward him, feelings that could lead nowhere. She wanted to hurl the accusation at him that his motives for wanting her were clearly understood, and just as clearly unappreciated. Since the conversation was disquieting, she pushed her chair away from the table and rose.

"Pray pardon me, milord. I'd like to retire. The day has been long."

He stood immediately. "You haven't answered my question, Margaret," he reminded her. "And this time be honest with both of us."

With her eyes kept purposely away from his face, she knew she was treading on dangerous ground; she could not lie. "That doesn't deserve an answer, milord," she said at last. Her lips were kept tight together to reinforce any temptation to be totally truthful about the condition of her heart. Margaret moved toward the stone stairway leading to the Great Hall and the rooms above. "My word doesn't change once I've given it," she assured him.

Climbing into bed, she thought about the nightly meetings in the kitchen and realized they were both a pleasure and a trial. Her heart strained at its bonds everytime she saw the young nobleman and sat in his presence. She had no recourse but to remain strong.

Late one morning in November, Gavin's uncle called Margaret to his chair by the fire in the Great Hall. "Your country has a new queen," he informed her.

"Mary Tudor is dead, milord?"

"She is. And Henry VIII's daughter, Elizabeth, is on the throne. But she has no right to be there," Lord Carlton said, pointing a finger to reinforce his statement. "Her father divorced his first wife and illegally married Anne, Elizabeth's mother, while his first wife was still living. Rightfully, our Regent's daughter, Mary—now in France with her husband—is the lawful Queen of both Scotland

and England. The young woman and her husband ought to claim that right immediately." Obviously satisfied that he had solved that sticky problem in his own way, Lord Carlton leaned back in his chair and pressed his lips tightly together.

Margaret wanted no part of a Scottish queen nor a French one. But the new Elizabeth might be more willing to aid the Reformers than the former ruler.

That night, as Robin was sewing Lord Carlton a wine-colored velvet doublet, with Margaret's help, Gavin repeated the news about the new queen. "You realize what this could mean to our cause, don't you, Robin?" he cried, enthusiasm ringing through his words.

Robin readily agreed, but his face took on a more somber look as he formed the words that followed. "Is it true that the Regent asked us to withdraw our petition for reform until Parliament meets?"

"Of course! I told the group she wasn't worthy of our trust, and now they know that what I said was true. The blasted woman is crafty as sin. She wants the jeweled crown of Scotland sent to her son-in-law in France as a Crown Matrimonial, and if she gets it accomplished, she has all France behind her to persecute us." Gavin paced nervously about the kitchen, a black scowl on his face. "She says she can't present two petitions at once—hers and ours. But we will pen another, a stronger one next time." He paused a moment, then spun around in fury. "We are being damned as heretics by that woman and her bishops!"

Margaret watched Gavin give a peat chip a mighty kick into the fireplace. His face, crimson with rage, matched the sparks of flame in his eyes. "Why doesn't Knox come back to Scotland?"

"He will, milord. When the time is right," assured Robin. Then he added quietly, knotting a thread and reaching for his scissors, "God has promised wisdom and patience if we ask it. Now excuse me, I must have a fitting with your uncle before he retires."

Lord Ballender glanced at Margaret as she reached for a shirt to mend. The firelight danced warm and soft on her long thick hair. Pliant folds of amber silk fitted snugly over her slender arms and waist and over the curves of her bodice. Though she and Gavin were alone, she did not take her eyes from the work occupying her. She couldn't trust herself to relax in his presence.

Gavin sat down next to her and stretched his legs out full length as he stared into the hot embers. "It will soon be Yuletide," he pointed out. "Are you content here at the mansion, Margaret? Do you have everything you need to keep warm?"

"It would do little good to be anything but content," she answered softly. "And, yes I am warm. The gowns your uncle supplied me are sufficient." Margaret placed the mended shirt on the table and reached for more thread.

"He is very fond of you, Margaret. In fact, I can safely say that you are the first woman of whom he has *ever* approved—other than his own wife."

"Knowing how beloved we English are to you, I should feel honored?" she challenged, daring him to answer her.

"You should, English or not." The fire's glow masked his skin with a handsome dark sheen that contrasted sharply with the sparkling brilliance of his teeth. "However, we shall see in future months how beloved your countrymen can be, assuming they are willing to help us."

"So am I to believe that anyone who is useful to you has a chance of being beloved?" Her tone was tartly accusing. She hastily tossed him a glance and reached for another shirt to mend.

"It helps. Although there are some rare exceptions."

The cold, damp days of January were shrouded with thick, penetrating fog that soaked through window sashes as would smoke, causing those inside the house to pull their wraps a little more tightly about them. The cook stirred the fire and lit small lamps to help combat the eerie, dense gloom of the dark morning hours.

The lamps' tiny illumination strove bravely to brighten the somber faces of Margaret and the servants as they breakfasted. When they finished, with no sign of Robin or Lord Ballender, Margaret voiced her concern.

The cook merely shrugged, and said, "They told me they wouldn't be here for several days."

"Where did they go?" Margaret persisted.

"They didn't say."

By midmorning the winter darkness began to drift into a pale dawn. Margaret continued her conjecture about Robin's and Gavin's whereabouts but could reach no satisfactory conclusion.

Lord Carlton called for her a few moments later. "Sit with me by the fire," he invited. "It's a depressing day. Our weather is horrid in the winter. We have so few hours of daylight and when this abominable fog settles in it's worse yet. This miserable Scottish weather is the only thing that doesn't change, it seems." He sighed and stared into the fire. His eyes studied the hot coals for several moments before he leaned forward and put his hands to the warmth. The blazing glow sent moving patterns on the paneled walls and the brightly painted beams overhead.

"In the great days of Scotland," he reflected, "the nobles of the land ruled the wealth of Scotland, along with the church. Now the rich merchants are taking over. They live and dress as we always did and they feel our equals, these brash fellows. Little wonder the wine merchant's daughter tries to snatch that young whelp of mine. She feels his equal." His scowl was black as the bricks behind the fire grate. "He needs a fine, stable well-bred wife to straighten him out. A woman like you, Margaret."

She listened with interest to the old man's account of the girl whom she'd seen in company with Gavin. "I am spoken for, milord," Margaret reminded him.

"So you think Corleal will wait for you? Nonsense. He doesn't even know where you are or if you are even alive." His lower lip pressed upward, moving the long gray beard of his chin at the same moment his hands folded firmly on the top of his walking stick. "Forget about him."

Margaret had no chance to reply; William announced a guest.

"It's Anson, no doubt. Stay where you are, Margaret. He's a friend and we have no secrets between us."

127

Lord Carlton greeted his friend, and asked for the news.

"A warning was posted on each monastery door demanding the friars to vacate so the poor of Scotland could move in."

"Who did such a thing?"

"It was signed in the name of the blind, crooked, widows, orphans, and all other poor. The warning claimed the friaries were endowed specifically to help the poor and needy, but instead, the friars are using the money to live on, while the poor share none of it."

"Is this true, Anson?"

The man nodded reflectively, his answer straightforward and simple. "It is true, yes. Their complaints are just. The Reformers have given the friars until Whitsunday, in May to comply."

Lord Carlton sat upright in his chair. "Then this amounts to revolution, Anson!"

"Ah, yes, but I'm beginning to wonder if the Reformers are not justified. Our Regent will not listen to the Scots' complaints and the Regent's church has a horribly disproportionate amount of wealth that could be used for the good of the country and our people. As it is, that wealth supports only the Regent's bishops and their families—and they have not been models of moral behavior. If it weren't for the rising merchant class of our land, our economy would be pitiable."

Lord Carlton shook his head sadly. "Why must things change, Anson?"

chapter
16

WHILE THE REGENT BREATHED out fiery threats of banishment for those who dared preach from the Scriptures, against her orders, rumor spread that she was taken seriously ill.

"A swelling of the legs," explained Robin to Margaret as they rode a couple of mares from Lord Carlton's stables, beyond the North Loch for exercise on a clear, cold day in January. "She fears neither God nor man for she has stated that so long as fame is hers, she cares not a whit for what God can do to her."

Margaret's eyes mirrored her inner shock. "The Regent truly said that?" she asked incredulously.

"She did. God doesn't look lightly on such vain babblings without meting out harsh judgment. It's a fearful thing to fall into the hands of the living God. Our Scot nobles have warned her what will happen if she refuses to listen to them, but still she turns a deaf ear. And to make matters worse, the young Mary, her daughter, and her French husband, have assumed the title of King and Queen of England and Ireland."

"Queen Elizabeth will not tolerate that at all," predicted Margaret gravely. "That amounts to treason."

"I know. The two of them plan to rule Scotland from their French throne, meaning of course, that we will be a puppet kingdom of France." Robin stared vaguely at some distant point without even seeing it. "You see, don't you, Margaret, our crucial position? If Scotland becomes a province of France, England will naturally be France's next conquest. No doubt Elizabeth is spewing out fire!"

Robin and Margaret pulled their horses to a stop and stared at the Edinburgh Castle on its high rocky projecture—rising, forbidding and lofty—above the North Loch. The winter sun drenched the ancient weathered stones of the fortress whenever it peeped from behind the blind of clouds long enough to do so.

Margaret studied the houses huddled along High Street, above the confines of the town walls, and the loch, beneath. The ancient stone walls sloped downward from the high castle perch toward the Holyrood Palace of the Regent at the far end of the town.

The dead foliage of winter covered the earth as a dull carpet, spreading across acres of fields shorn of their harvest's bounty. Above, the birds—sea gulls and kites—dipped in flight, as they searched for food. The drab gray of the barren rolling hills stretched as far as eye could see. Dark patches of deflowered, frost-stiffened gorse—and blackened heather—cloaked the nakedness of the austere scene with its myriads of sedgy pools, the result of abundant winter rains.

Margaret's thoughts unconsciously drifted away to thoughts of Chilton Manor and Corleal Castle.

"In England, we always celebrated Yule until Twelfth Night— the sixth of January," Margaret reminisced softly, a sigh escaping her lips. "I wonder if Lord Corleal remembered me when he lit his Yule log and brought in the boar's head to decorate his table."

"I'm sure he did, Margaret."

She immediately turned pleading eyes toward Robin before she continued.

"Can I not send a message by some means to let him know I'm safe—that I'll return to him one day—that I'm still alive?"

"Lord Ballender won't permit it."

"But why?" What could be Lord Ballender's excuse for refusing her request to contact her betrothed?

"I can't answer that, I'm afraid." Then in a conciliatory note he added, "You are treated well here, aren't you?"

"Regardless of how well I am treated, I am, Robin, a prisoner—a penniless prisoner." Margaret turned to stare into Robin's sober face. "When Lord Ballender decides to send me back, it may to be too late. Lord Corleal may be married to someone else by that time and then what will happen to me? Where will I go? I can't return to Chilton Manor, for it no longer belongs to me. I have no one. I have nowhere else to go but to Corleal. It's absolutely urgent that I contact him. I simply must!" The reality of her plight and her anxiety gained momentum and threatened to explode in frustration.

"Come, Margaret," urged Robin gently. "Let's ride. Trust God to work out your future, for he has something special for you that he will reveal to you in his own good time. Come," he repeated softly.

Dear Robin! Such wisdom God has given him! God exists in the fibers of his life, giving him the courage to face the future, black as it is for his countrymen, with the hope of an angel. Now he teaches me—I must trust God to solve my dilemma. But my patience is sorely tried!

Margaret and Robin rode eastward, beyond the North Loch, past the steeply rising Calton Hill, and followed the narrow, muddy road that led toward the seaport of Leith. From there they circled back again to the mansion. The outing was a welcome break from the duties to which she was bound.

The Regent's stern orders were issued in February. No meat was to be eaten during Lent and no disturbances were permitted against a pro-French religious service, on pain of death!

In spite of her orders, the Reformers kept pre-Pasch season as they believed God intended it kept. The Scottish preacher, Methuen, preached even more vigorously, rallying the people of Dundee behind the Reformers. John Willock again took over the pulpit in Edinburgh's St. Giles Church.

In the pale light of morning in early February, Margaret prepared to leave for services at St. Giles Cathedral. The black velvet of her gown brushed across the floor of the Hall as she moved toward Gavin waiting at the doorway with her heavy fur-lined cloak.

"You look most bonny in that gown, Margaret," he whispered, his hands lingering longer than necessary in the placing of the cloak about her shoulders.

"Please, milord, the servants—"

"The servants be hanged! I give the orders around here and I intend to do as I please!" His hands held her firmly in place. When Margaret turned her face from him, he forced her chin upward. "Look at me, Margaret," he commanded. Slowly her thick-lashed eyes stared into the black depths of his.

"If this were Saturday, I'd sweep you away to my chambers," he whispered, "and—"

"No, Gavin, you would not," she countered firmly. But she hoped her pounding heart did not sound as loudly in his ears as it did in hers. And that he could not read her thoughts. A small part of herself was alarmingly tempted to stay there with him in spite of her vocal refusal.

Robin limped with his crutch to the foot of the forestairs as he waited for Margaret and Gavin by the gate. When Margaret and Gavin came alongside, they all hurried off toward the kirk, their stools folded in the crooks of their arms. Margaret drew her furred cloak closely about her, for the wind swept across their bodies with icy blasts. Approaching the ancient stone kirk of St. Giles, Margaret studied the unusual lead roof of the spire—shaped like a royal crown—piercing the sky above the town pavement.

She turned to watch Robin move forward inside the cathedral. He placed his stool as near the pulpit as possible, while Gavin put both her stool and his along a rear pillar.

John Willock—the respected Scottish preacher—rose to the pulpit. Margaret saw in him a man as solemn and grave as ever a man walked. Immediately, a reverent hush fell over the Scots gathered there as he opened his mouth to speak. His speech relayed his intelligence, his education in letters and Scripture, his kindness, his assurance that God desired a people pure and undefiled by sin.

Margaret's eyes traveled from his small frame upward to the magnificent wood vaulting so far above the earthen floor that the heights seemed to brush against heaven itself. When her eyes lowered aimlessly, she discovered a pair of piercing chestnut eyes studying her. Sitting beneath the opposite pillar was the black-haired Betty, dressed in green velvet.

Her searing glance sent shudders down Margaret's back. Daggers of hatred spoke the merchant's daughter's resentment that Margaret was in the company of a man Betty regarded as her own personal property. If only she could turn toward Betty and declare the lack of attachments between herself and Gavin Ballender. Margaret found no pleasure in another's hatred.

When the service ended, Margaret noticed that several of the nobles sought Gavin as soon as they could force their way to where he stood. Lord Auchler relayed his news first. "The Regent's kirk council has enacted stiffer laws against our preachers, including John Willock himself."

"And that surprises you?" Gavin asked mockingly. "Did you expect the Regent's puppets to do less? The bitter anger of the people of Dundee brought that on, but it had to come, regardless of who started it."

"Also, we heard from John Knox," Auchler added. "Queen Elizabeth forbids his travel through England, unfortunately. We were hoping he could arrive in Scotland by way of the border. Now that's impossible. He did write, though, to encourage us to protect ourselves against these bloody tyrants. I'm alerting my soldiers to be ready to move out as soon as the order comes to march."

chapter
17

Gavin found Margaret in Lord Carlton's chambers, putting linens and clothes in order. "In the morning Robin is leaving on a preaching journey and I'll go along. I want you to go with us."

Margaret looked up from the pile of clothes that she had just searched for torn places to mend. She firmly shook her head. "But your uncle is unwell, milord. He's complained of pain and I cannot leave him. The doctor has asked me to make sure he rests and takes his medicine regularly."

Gavin smiled at Margaret as the firelight painted pink blushes on both her white skin and the gray silk of her gown. "You really like the old man, don't you?" he commented with amusement and interest.

"Yes. It's nice to belong, even if it is only temporary. And I must earn my keep. I don't flatter myself into thinking that I'm a guest in your uncle's house."

"He considers you one. You don't have to work."

"I prefer to keep busy. The time goes faster until I—"

"Until you can get away?" he countered dryly.

Margaret bit her lip but refused to look down. "If I don't, Lord Corleal will no longer have me and I have no one else to go to. Surely, sir, you can understand that and you won't keep me here much longer." Margaret looked up at the man with a tension choked throat, but she refused to yield to tears. Her voice was bitter in its accusation toward him. "How can you be so cruel?"

Gavin placed his strong hands on Margaret's shoulders and looked into her pain-filled eyes. "Margaret, listen to me." He talked directly to her even though she kept her eyes stubbornly averted. "My men accidentally frightened your family's horses. It was not intended, I swear it. They felt they couldn't leave you there, for Corleal would have burned our village as sure as I stand here. I can't tell you which side stole horses and cattle first—or even how many years ago it began—but I do know that what we took was ours. Then Robin and I found we needed you. We still do. Now my uncle needs you, too. He is, as I said, very fond of you." Gavin gently smoothed the hair from Margaret's forehead and waited impatiently for her to look up at him.

"But what you don't seem to—or care to—understand, milord, is that I promised to marry the Lord of Corleal. He asked me to be his wife. At least I would belong there." She hesitated a moment only, her teeth chewing in agitation on the flesh of her mouth before she continued. "As it is, I belong nowhere."

"Do you love him?" Gavin pursued stubbornly, refusing to accept such an explanation as final.

Margaret refused to answer.

"Look at me," he ordered sternly.

She raised her lids and long lashes to glance slowly into his piercing black eyes. "Does it matter to you—since you're determined to keep me from going to him?"

"It matters to me, yes," he whispered. "More than you think." His fingers tightened on her shoulders, aware of the trembling reaction she attempted to hide. "Margaret," Gavin murmured softly, "marry me and forget about your promise to a man you don't love. I promise I will make you happy. And you will belong here with me." His face lowered so that his lips came in contact with her cheek, brushing the skin lightly.

Margaret drew back, facing him squarely, an accusing look in her blue eyes. "To save your inheritance. That's why you ask me, isn't it?" she demanded impatiently, pride moving her chin a fraction higher. Then turning around, with the few pairs of hose to be

136

mended still in her hand, she swept from the room before he could respond and witness the tears of frustration and humiliation forming once again in her eyes. Not only was she promised, she was aware that Gavin's life was totally void of any commitment to God.

After Robin and Gavin left before daylight with their soldiers, Margaret walked to the third floor to look out over the barren land that would soon bloom with spring freshness. She pictured both men riding forth with the excitement of adventure emblazoned across the face of one and the godly words of the Scriptures glowing from the face of the other.

Then Margaret's thoughts unconsciously swerved to the raven-haired beauty, Betty Stanus. Did Gavin take her along this time, when she, herself, refused to go? Would she comfort him at night? Sleep in his arms?

She paced restlessly through the house to still her whirling emotions. Then in a flash, she rebuked herself with the admonition, "Neither of them means anything to me. All Gavin Ballender wants of me is the means to saving his inheritance." But even as she reminded herself of the reason behind his proposal, she could not dismiss him so easily as that. Nor could she deny the hurt her reasoning inflicted.

Would she truly be able, she asked herself miserably, to forget Lord Ballender when she was finally returned to Corleal?

Margaret's steps brought her closer to the window—without her realization. She opened it and stared out over the North Loch to the runrigs beyond, where villagers turned the deadened dregs of winter beneath their plows in preparation for spring planting.

It was now ten months since she had been taken and since her father— Here Margaret closed her eyes in remembrance of the horrible scene as if it were yesterday. She forced herself to close the window and retrace her steps to the first floor of the house and to busy herself in an attempt at keeping her mind occupied with more worthwhile thoughts.

The long clock chimed its tinkling little reminder of the hour and Margaret knew it was time for Lord Carlton's medicine. When she walked into the Great Hall with her bottle and a glass of water, she found him with the same visitor who had called upon the old man before.

"You remember my housekeeper, Anson?"

The man flashed a hasty glance of recognition Margaret's way. "Yes, I remember."

"I'm reduced to taking medicine for my health, it seems," Lord Carlton offered lamely. "Deuced vile stuff." Turning to Margaret he ordered, "Put it here on the table for a few minutes, my dear, and sit down. I don't want to spoil my conversation just yet." The old man motioned to a chair near him and shifted his attention back to his visitor.

"Now, Anson, continue." He gave a sharp, impatient flick of his finger. "You realize I'd know nothing if you didn't keep me informed of events. That nephew of mine seldom sits down long enough to tell me anything. And when he does, he feels obliged to argue. The young fool. Went off yesterday for who knows where." Then, as if he remembered that Anson had come to share the latest news, he motioned for him to proceed. "But go on."

Anson settled back in his chair and sighed. "The Regent is finally dealing a blow to these heretics, for she has put five of them to the horn."

"Good," Lord Carlton conceded with satisfaction. "Now maybe that will end the violence. That's what they deserve for their blatant audacity in posting that summons on the friars' door in January."

"It might here in Edinburgh, but not in other parts of the country. The violence seems to be gaining momentum in the villages and towns elsewhere."

"Yes. These lawbreakers will find that the Regent has strong military support if they push further."

Anson sighed. "Yes, I'm afraid they will."

"Fools! All of them!" acidly spat out the old man. "Why can't they just be content with things as they were?"

"Ah, my friend," Anson shook his head sadly in response, "that's just it. Things have not been as they used to for some time. The

French soldiers the Regent has brought in among us are not models of good behavior. Our Scottish noblemen are becoming angrier. That's evident."

"But it's certainly not grounds for heresy! If our people would try to understand the woman and cooperate—"

"You have been shut away too long, I see," Anson interrupted. "Even I can see the faults there. No, my friend, our heretic friends have just cause."

Lord Carlton sent an accusing look toward his old friend, a darkening scowl of disbelief and anger surfacing. "Do I detect a changing loyalty in you, Anson?" he demanded. "I'm shocked to hear you talk like this."

"I admit nothing," said the man in defense of his comments. "I will say, though, that if this exile—this John Knox—ever comes back here and gives leadership to these badly frayed Reformers, there will be a clash that we will wish we never witnessed."

"The man wouldn't dare return. I wonder if this fool, Knox, was ever told that the Regent's clergy burned him in effigy after he left Scotland? No doubt they'd be more than happy to burn the real thing!"

Margaret learned that the Scottish preacher, Paul Methuen, was put to the horn—outlawed for his disobedience in preaching publicly after the Regent made demands against such speaking. The Regent's bishops had called a meeting to fight the Scripture preaching among the Scottish preachers and vowed to stop it.

The Reformers drew up a retaliatory petition. Gavin asked Margaret to carefully write it on parchment to present to the Regent.

"Sir James Sandilands of Calder has been asked to present it at the next meeting of Parliament," Gavin informed Margaret by way of explanation. "He is old, walks straight and tall, and commands reverence. Besides, he's perfectly honest in all his dealings. His faithful obedience to authority makes him beyond reproach.

"All he asked," added Gavin, pacing restlessly about as he

proceeded with his reasoning, "is that the woman listen to him about our need for public worship as we see fit and that she forbids any more burnings." He pursed his lips and let out a frustrated sigh. "I personally think we are wasting our time, but, unfortunately, I was outvoted in this."

The bands of Reformers met frequently to take counsel with one another, to fast and pray. Robin, with Margaret accompanying, met in homes of those who wished it and gave comfort and sermon exhortation to stay close to God, waiting on the supreme guidance of the One whose wisdom must be sought above all else.

"The bishops storm in protest," gloated Gavin, "but the more they repress us, the stronger our people band together."

With longer days of spring and the air less chilling, Margaret eagerly opened the windows to take advantage of occasional patches of sun. Everywhere she saw fresh green touches of new growth lying as a soft carpet spread over the runrigs and distant hills as far as her eyes could see. The runrigs were interspersed with wild patches of daffodils and thick tangles of brambles on the slope. Reaching to the loch, they were suddenly transformed from a dead heap to a delicate film of color.

The week before Pasch, Margaret consented to go to the market place alone. Without the Ballender soldiers' help, the household was again understaffed and the cook needed supplies of salt and vinegar.

Margaret walked steadily along toward High Street. The bell tolled for selling to begin and the housewives moved, as did she, to purchase necessities for their families. She slowed her pace when she approached the cloth shop and stopped a moment to examine a piece of fine wool. When someone bumped her from behind, Margaret turned hastily, looking up into the face of Betty Stanus.

The young woman made no apology for the rough contact, speaking so softly that only Margaret's ears caught the message she relayed.

"Meet me in St. Giles Kirk in a few minutes." And without

looking at Margaret, she moved on, obviously confident that her supposed rival would comply to her demands without questioning them.

Curiosity overcame Margaret's fear of walking into the dark close alone. Margaret followed between a quaint row of buildings—all heavily eaved—and passed through the Auld Kirk Stile Close to the North Porch entrance of St. Giles Kirk. Her heart beat rapidly as she moved into the dark chancel of the cathedral and waited silently for her eyes to adjust to the dimly lit interior.

Betty was carefully hidden under a hood and cloak and did not turn until she heard a soft voice behind her.

"You wish to speak to me?" Margaret questioned, letting her presence be known.

Betty swung around and studied Margaret with interest. She demanded brusquely, "You came alone?"

"Yes."

A smile curved Betty's lips into a mocking pose. "You, no doubt, want to return to England?"

"Why do you ask?" Margaret eyed the woman with increased suspicion.

"Because I can arrange for you to go back to Corleal. I'm sure you don't like being held prisoner here."

Margaret's heart pounded at the offer. Here was the opening for which she had waited, for eleven long months, not expecting an opportunity to appear in such an unexpected way. "Go on," she admonished her with rising interest.

Betty lifted her proud head and looked disdainfully at the girl beside her. "Lord Ballender will make me his wife one day after the estates are his. We are lovers and have been for some time. I am aware that his uncle does not approve of me, but Gavin will never give me up. *Never!*" The words exploded from her lips. "Even if he would be forced to marry another woman, I would continue to be his paramour. He would insist on that."

Margaret gazed at the churlish curl of Betty's lip and the elevated height of her chin while the woman spoke out so blatantly. That

Betty spoke the truth, she had little doubt, but Margaret resented the brazen words coming from the woman's vile tongue. Even so, she carefully held her peace.

"My father is wealthy and I am a lady just as much as you," Betty challenged unwaveringly. Her eyes swept over the fine velvet of Margaret's dress and the ermine trim of her cloak with haughty disdain before she continued.

Too angry to answer such folly from so uncouth an individual as Betty Stanus, she would not give the woman the satisfaction of knowing the extent of the deep antagonism she was causing.

If Betty sensed annoyance, she chose to ignore it, pursuing her precisely aimed, barbed comments as an old bent man moved nearer, interrupting Betty's purpose of secrecy, keeping his face down to study his carefully placed steps. The woman lowered her voice to a whisper.

"Meet my maidservant here in the kirk early on the morning of May tenth and give her a letter for Lord Corleal, signed by you. I will see to its safe delivery by one of my men." Then stopping, Betty looked directly at Margaret. "Tell no one of this," she warned, "for I will deny I ever talked to you if you do. Is this perfectly clear?"

"Very." Betty Stanus gave a slight nod, then turned and disappeared through the opposite doorway from which she'd entered moments before. Margaret leaned weakly against the thick Norman pillar that helped support the high vaulted ceiling, her mind a whirl of confusion and emotion. How did Betty know so much about her? Who told the woman about Lord Corleal?

Pushing herself upright, Margaret walked toward the spice stall on High Street. Betty Stanus had claimed Gavin as her own; Margaret knew she could be speaking the truth. After all, she herself had seen them together—they had seemed content. And perhaps she spoke the truth, too, about Gavin's fidelity—or lack of it. Margaret's lips tightened.

The second day of May was cloudy but bright. The sun shone on the fresh spring green of the plum trees and pear trees. Breezes swept through the green shoots of grain on the runrigs and the waving pasture grasses on the hillsides.

Margaret helped Robin put the finishing stitches to a Holland linen shirt and assisted Gavin into it to see if it fit properly. While he modeled the finished garment, William informed him that a visitor had arrived.

Lord Auchler didn't wait for an invitation but burst into the room with his eyes afire, impatiently waiting for the servant to depart before he spoke.

"What is it?" Gavin prodded. "Speak up!"

"John Knox has arrived!" He blurted out the news in breathless gasps.

"When?" Gavin practically leaped to Auchler's side.

"A short while ago. But I needn't warn you to keep it quiet for the Regent will have him arrested if she hears of it. She's still raging because he eluded her grasp before, slipping away before she could have him burned."

"Do you realize what this means?" Gavin demanded. "We begin in earnest now, for Knox knows the country is ripe for Reform and for ridding ourselves of these French locusts!"

In the semi-darkness of the room Margaret observed the fiery excitement Gavin exuded. He was undeniably handsome. She thought of his lips, smiling smiles that melted her entire frame. Then she pictured Betty and him together. The thought of the dark-haired woman made her shudder. Would Gavin be angry that his inheritance had been torn out from under him if Corleal should come for her? She refused to consider how she, herself, would feel when she finally left Gavin behind, never to see him again, and returned to England with her betrothed.

On Wednesday night, Gavin waited for Margaret in the kitchen while she helped the cook put the room in order. "Come to me in the orchard," he directed softly. "I will wait under the first plum tree." Before she had the opportunity to object, he turned about and hurried up the steps, taking them by twos until he reached the top.

Margaret approached the rendezvous spot sometime later and was startled to feel his arm casually slip around her shoulders. He spoke in quiet tones only the two of them could hear.

"We are going to accompany Knox to Dundee in the morning and you are going along." Detecting that she was about to refuse, he hurried on. "There are enough servants to take care of my uncle, so you have no excuse for staying here."

"I cannot leave." Her thoughts trailed back to Betty and the promised letter. That message had to be at the kirk on the tenth if it were to be delivered to Lord Corleal. This was her only remaining chance to contact her betrothed and return to her homeland and him.

"Could it be that you have other plans? Hm?" Margaret remained silent, her heart racing. Lord Ballender swung her around to observe her face in the waning light of evening. "Look at me." His directive was stern as iron.

She raised her eyes to meet his, waiting for his questions.

"Who did you meet at the kirk while I was gone?"

It seemed impossible that he should know. She had seen no one except one old man.

"Who was she?" he persisted. "Tell me."

"Why did you think I met someone?" She purposely stalled for time, not wanting to tell him the answer.

"Because William followed you."

"I cannot tell you." Margaret tried unsuccessfully to pry loose from his firm grasp on her.

"Then let me guess. The woman approached you at the cloth stall and you followed her to the kirk. She was taller than you, with black hair. What did she want? Answer me!" he demanded harshly. Margaret's stubborn refusal to reply only triggered further wrath. "She wants to help you return to England. Am I right?" Gavin's eyes were blazing firebrands as he watched her reaction to his probing.

"I shall not answer you."

"Then I'm right. She wants you away from here."

"What difference does it make, milord?" Margaret challenged, a flatness overriding her accusations. "You're only afraid of losing your inheritance if I leave."

"That, my love, doesn't deserve an answer, either," he tossed back, not fully denying her charges. He seized her and wrapped his arms about her before she realized what was happening. He lowered his lips to hers in a lightning-quick flash that left her reeling. When his face drew back to search the blue of her eyes, he warned, "Corleal would not kiss you like that."

"Perhaps not," she flung her words at him, pushing against the solid wall of his chest to be released, "but mine would be the only ones he'd kiss!"

"I can see," he warned mockingly, holding her at arm's length, "that you are in for a shock. Corleal is not the paragon of virtue you think."

chapter

18

GAVIN COMMANDED MARGARET to mount a gray horse as the first streaks of dawn washed across the sky. The retinue—Robin, Margaret, Gavin, Lord Auchler, a few servants and two companies of soldiers—raced along the shoreline of the Firth of Forth from the seaport of Leith and headed west until they approached a party moving ahead of them in the pale light of morning.

The lead horse carried a stern-looking little man with an air of full authority in his straight carriage. His shoulders were broad, his hair black beneath a flat hat. A dark beard hung to his chest. His countenance, whenever visible to Margaret, was one of grave sternness. Without being told, she felt sure the horseman was the man who had secretly arrived in the country the night before: John Knox. No doubt he was happy to get as far away from Edinburgh as possible since the bishop and Regent would consider him a prime candidate for burning.

The group proceeded along the south bank of the long island bay and ferried across at the narrowest neck of water to the northern shore. The rolling hills were barren except for the dark patches of gorse and spiny slivers of broom breaking the stark outlines.

As the party moved steadily northward toward the town of Dundee, Margaret thought about Betty Stanus. She could imagine the woman's anger if the appointment was not kept as planned and there was no note to carry to Lord Corleal. Would Betty contact

Lord Corleal, without a signed note? Margaret prayed that she would.

Margaret realized she was the only woman in the retinue heading north. The others surely must think her a servant, dressed as she was in her plain, coarse garment of wool beneath her cloak.

The group members displayed a united purpose in cause, speaking grimly of the coming confrontation. Incident after incident was relayed, in the order of its happening, to bring John Knox up to date about the events that had taken place before his arrival in Scotland. Finally, he was informed of the Regent's demand for the Reformers to meet her at Stirling Castle in one week.

When Margaret got her first view of Dundee in the distance, faint sunset was brushing the sky. Margaret studied the town hugging the coast of the Firth of Tay as a child is clasped to its mother's breast. The procession moved past the long fish market and circled the Castle Hill, arriving at last in the center of town.

By the next day, a large assembly of Reformers had gathered in the kirk of Dundee to elect John Knox the leader of their great cause. The enormous brows above John's eyes raised in unison with the motion of his long narrow fingers as he urgently sought the assembly to seek God's direction in ridding their land of the French and gaining freedom from persecution for their faith in Christ.

From her seat in the rear of the kirk, Margaret watched the group elect the calm-natured man, Erskine—the Laird of Dun—to precede it to Stirling Castle with the purpose of informing the Regent that even though their gathering was large, they were coming in peace to meet with her as commanded.

"The choice of Erskine was a good one," Robin commented afterward. "He is a gentle, godly man and if anyone can talk to the Regent, he can. He's not easily provoked."

"True," Gavin said, skepticism overshadowing his agreement, "but he will not be dealing with a rational woman, and I do not feel good about *that*."

By the eighth of May, the large gathering of Reformers turned their faces in the direction of the town of St. Johnston. Margaret realized, with a sinking heart, that she would not be returning to Edinburgh in time to meet at the kirk with Betty's maid. *O Lord,* she pleaded silently, accompanying Robin toward the next town, *help me to have the faith to believe you will solve my situation in your own time. Help me to remain patient and accept each day as it comes.*

With the walls of St. Johnston ahead in the distance, the Reformers talked of nothing but the coming summons of the Regent, two days hence. They moved in a direct line toward the town. The high ground on which they traveled melted into flat and level terrain, the nearer they came to the town wall. The surrounding land was green with spring grasses and dotted with sheep and new lambs gamboling about on their long, spindly legs. With an open mouth, the shepherd stared at the procession. His sheep ceased their nibbling long enough to turn curious black faces toward the passing parade, then in their quiet way resumed feeding.

Margaret rode alongside Robin in company with the huge procession entering the town of St. Johnston by way of an arched bridge. Soon, Knox's words of exhortation rumbled throughout the great pillared St. Johns Kirk, warning that the coming battle would be great, but the focus and target of their fight was freedom of both faith and country.

When the great gathering mounted horses and started on its mission to Stirling Castle two days later, it was met by a returning Erskine bringing word from the Regent that the Reformers were not to appear as bidden, but were to wait in St. Johnston for further notice. He did not pretend to understand the reason for the change of plans, but begged them to be obedient and acquiescent.

Margaret heard Gavin's spontaneous protest. "Why? Her summons was explicit; be there on the tenth. Why the sudden switch?" His query was tinged with angry misgiving and suspicion. "Let us go on, I say!" A sharp division of opinion among the band followed, but Erskine urged everyone, in his gentle way, to do as the woman commanded. "Let us concede on this small request in order to keep peace."

The waiting was interminable; the mood explosive. When, on the following morning, Erskine rode in to announce that the Regent had cunningly outlawed the entire gathering for not appearing before her the previous day, his otherwise placid nature burst with fury at the blatantly outrageous deception.

"The wretched woman!" Gavin exploded. "Let her rot!"

The huge gathering of infuriated Reformers listened to an impassioned sermon that afternoon, then began to decry the Regent's abominable treachery. One young man, angered with the Regent and the clergy, cried out against a priest at the far side of the kirk. Instantly, the priest seized the young man and soundly boxed his ears. In livid retaliation, the boy loosened a rock from the ground at his feet and hurled the missile, striking one of the statues near the priest. Onlookers needed no further encouragement to do likewise, and began to loosen stones and vent their rage until every statue in the huge kirk lay strewn on the floor.

Still smarting from the Regent's deception, the inflamed mob of townspeople moved into the streets, gathering momentum and supporters from every direction.

Margaret clung to Robin as Knox and the nobles tried to calm the mob. But it was as useless as putting a wet cloth to a burning house. She and Robin were swept along, unable to turn back. The fury of betrayal was directed toward the monasteries beyond the town walls. Long had the abuses and frustrations of the common people gone unheeded. Here, at last, was a chance for revenge. They broke through the gates and swarmed into the friary, shocked at the provisions in store inside the storerooms. Puncheons of salt beef, casks of wine, costly napery, and coverlets were dragged into the open.

"The hypocrites!" the people shouted, their condemnation sharpened at the sight of the food. "While the rest of us starve under unreasonable taxes, the friars feast on hoarded food! They constantly profess poverty and wear long faces to fool us with false piety! Hypocrisy!" the mob stormed.

For two days Margaret stayed close to Robin and watched the

common lot burn the ancient buildings until nothing but the walls remained. Orchards were cut to the ground. Storerooms were sacked and food carried away.

"Although I don't condone this destruction," observed Robin, "I can't begrudge the common lot their booty after years of abuse. It suffices somewhat for the misery they've endured."

"What will the Regent say to all this?" asked Margaret fearfully.

"Only God knows," answered Robin, shaking his head sadly.

Within two days the answer came from an enraged Regent. She vowed to send her army to burn the whole town of St. Johnston and spread salt on the ground to render it fruitless.

Margaret felt the pervading blaze of anger against a Regent whose word meant nothing, and lent her hand to help Lord Ballender and Robin with the Reformers to ready themselves against the Regent's French army—reportedly ten miles away. The army was sure to storm the town of St. Johnston in retaliation for the riots and destruction of the monasteries.

With the sinking of the sun in the west came a rise in tension and uncertainty as to what the enemy would do when it arrived the next day.

Gavin walked in the garden behind the house where he, Margaret, and Robin stayed. "The numbers are increasing for our cause," he informed Margaret. "We will gather outside town on the morrow to wait for the enemy's arrival. Since Robin's crippled leg won't do well in battle, he will be back and forth between the field and the town with messages." Lord Ballender's arm slipped around Margaret's waist as they approached the wall at the rear of the garden. "I don't know what will happen in the coming days, but I want you to promise me you will not slip away from us and try to escape."

"That's highly unlikely, milord," she responded dryly. "Where would I go? We're a long way from Edinburgh."

Lord Ballender purposely ignored her acid comments. "I asked you to marry me awhile back," he reminded her. "Do you remember that, Margaret?"

"Yes, I remember." Her heart accelerated with his nearness and his referral to the marriage proposal, but she kept her voice calm despite her trembling body. "You know my answer," she whispered stoically.

"Perhaps one day you will change your mind," Gavin countered softly, drawing her unyielding body closer to his side.

The following morning, Margaret stood at the wharf to watch both Gavin and Robin ride out with the soldiers under the blazing banner of Ballender, their long spears gleaming in the sun, swords at their sides. For as long as she could see, she studied Gavin's straight, muscled outline, his face not veering from the direction of the expected French army. She felt a sudden rush of despair. "Lord, be with them," Margaret whispered.

Once again she relived the pleasure of his gentle attentions toward her and the words telling her he wanted to marry her. But his true feelings for her—his motives—remained unclear. He had never denied the fact that he had to marry a lady to rescue his inheritance. But she was not free to encourage him, either, Margaret reminded herself, watching the disappearing figures beneath the proudly fluttering blue and white banner.

During the day, Margaret felt the oppression of her assigned room intolerable, and left it to walk aimlessly about. But she found herself wishing, as she walked, that she had stayed home. *Home?* What was home now? Did she mean her father's house, or Lord Carlton's?

She moved about the shop stalls and wandered down quaint wynds awhile before moving on to the town wharf. Small sailing boats were arriving and delivering their catches at the fish market nearby, with daily life continuing, as it had for centuries, in spite of the fact that just a short distance away, men stood in readiness to do battle for their country and their beliefs, as well as for their lives. Margaret marveled at the constant flow of the water, as unceasing as the love of God, an endless stream of mercy and love.

Turning suddenly, she saw Robin approaching through the city gates, riding in the company of seven men. He escorted three nobles, in the company of four French soldiers, as they moved warily along the stone pavement toward the house where Knox was gathered with several of the Reformers' leaders. Margaret guessed that the men came to discuss grievances and try to come to some sort of an agreement.

That night, at supper, a grave Gavin turned to Margaret and informed her of his plans. "I can't take you out in the field with us, naturally, for it's too dangerous. We expect fighting in the morning, so I've made arrangements for you to stay here in town with a family of one of our men. I'll take you there first thing in the morning before we ride out to camp and then I'll be sure you're safe."

With dawn washing the sky amber, Gavin—true to his word—took Margaret to the house in town. He helped her dismount, then held on to her arm to relay a few last instructions. "Promise me you'll not leave the house unless you are accompanied by Mistress Murray or a trusted servant of the family."

"I promise," she answered quietly.

The gaze of Gavin's dark eyes unnerved Margaret to the point of wishing that he truly loved her for herself—no inheritance conditions attached—and no Betty, no Corleal. How happy she could be basking in his love alone. Then as if he read her thoughts, she colored deeply while Gavin pulled her close to him and planted a parting kiss on her forehead.

"Come," he said softly, "and we'll get you settled."

A servant showed the pair into the hall where Anna Murray and her son, Walter, pored over a book at a large oak table. They rose immediately to welcome their guest, then stood quietly while Lord Ballender took his leave with, "You are in good hands, Margaret, but remember your promise to me."

A servant pulled an extra chair to the fire and prepared for a light meal from the livery cupboard. While the three ate, Margaret noticed the nervous servants snatching glances from the second-story windows down to the street below as if they expected trouble. Walter joined them, standing behind a curtain to watch. Before long he relayed excitedly, "Look! The Regent and her French lieges are crossing the bridge and coming into our town!"

Anna rose with Margaret and stood beside Walter. "She's come to see the destruction, no doubt. I'm told the Regent was very upset about the burning of Charterhouse. The building was old and a favorite of her husband. It was burned when the friaries went up in smoke."

Margaret's hands formed a tight little knot and her pulse rose. She felt a deep apprehension at the sight of the Regent and her soldiers in the town, in violation of her day-old promise that she would not station them there. With haste the Regent's retinue turned and followed the route leading to the monasteries beyond the town. They were soon out of sight, beyond the town walls.

"I feel certain that they will be back," Anna warned, "and soon." The woman picked up her needlework and made quick nervous stitches, while the rest of the family watched the wynd below.

"She vowed to kill all of us," Walter reminded everyone present, fear showing in his large eyes. "Do you think she'll really do it, Mother?"

"I doubt she'd be that foolish since our army is stationed not far beyond the town." None of Anna's encouraging words forfeited the numbing apprehension that seeped into the hearts of all the occupants in the house as they watched from the second story. They all knew the treacherous Regent couldn't be trusted.

"Here they come!" At Walter's shout, Margaret immediately rushed toward the window as the soldiers spread in all directions as a spider's web, moving straight toward the houses of the Reformers' town leaders before stopping.

When the first volley of ammunition exploded, all the hysterical servants ran screaming to the living quarters on the second floor. "They're firing on us!"

Margaret gasped in horror as the shot hit Walter, tossing him into a crumpled heap on the floor. Anna leaped from her chair, her face ashen as she knelt by the lifeless body of her son. "O God," she cried out in anguish, "not my son!" The inhumanity of the horrible

154

incident was over in a matter of seconds, leaving everyone stunned and shaken while the enemy soldiers and the Regent escaped unharmed across the bridge.

When word of the tragedy reached camp, Gavin and the nobles stormed into the town, vowing that the Regent would pay dearly for this day's treachery. Lord Ballender raced up the steps of the house, two at a time. After he offered his condolences to Anna Murray, he gathered Margaret into his arms. She wept openly on his shoulder.

"Thank God you're safe," he muttered over and over again, holding her tightly against him. "Because of the miserable Regent's lies stating that she wouldn't bring soldiers into the town, five of her important officers have left her and come to join our forces. It doesn't make up for what the rotten creature did to this boy, but it's a taste of what's to come!" he vowed through clenched teeth. His face was a mask of deep hatred. "The cursed woman had the audacity to say she was sorry the boy's father wasn't the victim!"

Then, pressing Margaret even closer, he stated firmly, "You'll stay in Robin's and my tent tonight and I'll not let you out of my sight again until we're back in Edinburgh."

With a backdrop of early morning mists making the surrounding hills obscure, the Reformers watched Lord James Stuart and the Earl of Argyll—two of the men who defected from the enemy camp the day before—mount up to ride toward the direction of St. Johnston and on to St. Andrews on the North Sea, with the purpose of enlisting aid for the Reformers.

Gavin watched with pleasure as the two men rode off into the fog. "They go to set up a Reformation in the very town where Walter Miln was burned for his simple faith in God. They'll go about the shires to raise support for our cause. As yet, all the towns and villages haven't been reached." With a smile pushing up the corners of his mouth and dark mustache, Lord Ballender hurried on. "How lucky we are to have those two. Our victory is sure now! We will follow and join them four days hence."

He turned back to the young woman at his side. "When I think how close you came to being killed by those rotten Frenchmen, my blood boils."

Margaret felt her heart race with the ring of his words—words of concern for her safety—but a needling doubt caused her to wonder if the statement was prompted by the thought of his inheritance slipping through his fingers, like water, or if it was a true anxiety for her welfare.

"But I wasn't, milord. God took care of me."

chapter
19

THE BATTLE CRY against the French gathered momentum as the Reformers pulled down their tents and headed in the direction of the eastern seacoast towns of Scotland. Their mission focused on making villagers and townsmen everywhere aware of the French menace and deceit of the Regent and on rallying forces—under the leadership of Knox—against that enemy.

From atop his stallion, Gavin studied Margaret on the gray mount next to his. "Do you miss my uncle?" he questioned her.

"Yes, I do. I liked the feeling of being settled in one place and having plenty to do to pass my time. He was kind to me after he knew I was not your mistress."

"You *could* be my mistress, Margaret. I would be good to you. And he would never know."

"You are mistaken," she responded, her words bristling with underlying indignation. "I could not, nor would I ever be a man's mistress!"

Gavin laughed. "I knew you'd say that." Then sobering instantly he added, "I thank God that you're safe. I was frantic when I rode in from camp yesterday not knowing if you'd been hit, too." He eyed her a moment before commenting, "You've been in Scotland a year now."

"Yes," Margaret sighed. Little had she known, when she had left Chilton, that she'd never see it again or that she would never reach

Lord Corleal's castle. But she was equally sure that whatever happened to her, she had that settled peace which kept her—and would continue to keep her—in the perilous days ahead.

Margaret's golden hair blew wild in the cool breezes and when she glanced at Gavin, he smiled at her and guided his horse closer. "You have seen more of Scotland than anyone else in the whole of your England will ever see in his lifetime."

"I cannot deny that."

"Are you sorry, Margaret?" Gavin continued questioning softly.

Margaret reflected before commenting. "That remains to be answered."

The day following, the lords and Knox gathered in the kirk of Anstruther on the northern side of the Firth of Forth. The occurrences at St. Johnston were repeated. The people needed little encouragement to vent their hatred against an immoral, uncaring pro-French clergy that exacted fees by preying on the fears of the common people for tithes.

The sky was a pale blue, dotted with myriads of racing cloud puffs. Dozens of gulls flew low over the rocks searching for food. The rolling waves, roaring in from the North Sea, smashed against the crags of the east coast of Scotland, bringing with them the scents of fish and salt spray.

Margaret gazed pensively out over the great expanse of ocean wondering if she would ever see her homeland again. Her blond hair blew wild in the strong breezes that whipped savagely across white-capped waves. It was useless to try to stop the strands from catching on her lashes. Her cloak swirled about her legs. Even after a year, Margaret realized her future was as hazy and uncertain as when she had been taken captive on the way to her wedding.

For the next few days, the Reformers accompanied John Knox as he preached in the kirks along the east coast.

Early Saturday afternoon an exuberant procession headed toward St. Andrews. Margaret rode near enough to Knox to detect a glint of anticipation in his deep blue eyes. She had learned that his vow, since being taken prisoner from St. Andrews twelve years before, was to preach the love of God in that kirk again one day.

When the group neared the town of St. Andrews, a rider swung into view along the ancient road and reined his mount to a halt. "Milords," he informed those at the head of the procession, "Knox's presence is needed immediately in town. If you will follow me, sir, I will take you there."

He would say no more as to the emergency of the summons, so the group had little choice but to keep steady pace behind the rider, speculating as to his intent.

Lord Ballender bid a hasty good-by, with the parting words that Robin was to take Margaret to the inn and wait for him there. Then he turned his stallion about to accompany the others as they preceded the remaining retinue into town.

Margaret felt a wash of alarm as she turned to Robin and voiced her qualms. "Why do you suppose they are so anxious to have Mr. Knox in town?"

Robin looked ahead at the disappearing horsemen, answering without so much as turning his head toward Margaret. "It's difficult to determine that. I do know that the Bishop of St. Andrews is the Regent's stepson," he added, sharing that bit of pertinent information, "but I also know that the Regent and that stepson are not on friendly terms. But God will keep John Knox safe, regardless."

Arriving in town, Robin directed Margaret to follow him. "We'll get settled at the inn and wait for Gavin's return. We have no idea how long that meeting at Lord James's will take."

Later that night, one of Lord James's servants lit Gavin's way from his master's house to the inn where Robin and Margaret sat by the fire discussing the present perils facing the Reformers. He swung into the inn, loosening his mantle and throwing it down on the seat of a high-backed chair near the fire.

Margaret and Robin waited silently, expectantly, to hear the full report of the urgency.

"That viper, the Bishop of St. Andrews, is in town and has sent word to Lord James and the Earl of Argyll warning that if John Knox preaches in his cathedral tomorrow, he will be facing a dozen French culverins aimed straight at his nose." Gavin's lips stretched taut over his teeth in gnawing agitation. "Naturally some of the weak-kneed nobility among us tried to talk Knox out of preaching tomorrow. They're actually afraid!"

"So what's going to happen now?" Robin interrupted, excitement lacing his words.

"They called in Knox, himself, to make that decision." Lord Ballender rose and paced before the fire, his mouth curled up in a sly smile. "What is he going to do?" A short triumphant laugh escaped his lips. "I'll tell you what he's going to do—and I know now—if I didn't know it before—why he is our leader instead of another. Aha! You should have heard him, Robin; I tell you, you missed a prize!

"Despite efforts to persuade Knox otherwise, the fellow stood and faced us all with those piercing eyes of his. He said, without so much as lowering his chin an inch, 'God is my witness that I never preached Christ in contempt of any man, in fear of my own safety or to the hurt of anyone. But, gentlemen, delaying preaching I refuse to do and still keep a good conscience.

"'In this town and church,' he thundered, 'God first called me to the dignity of preaching! It was from this very place—this cathedral—that I was taken away by the tyranny of France—because of the bishops—as you all know. It's not the time to tell you in detail how long I was a prisoner and how many torments I endured at their hands as a galley slave—or the heartaches that resulted from it. But this one thing I can't hide, and more than one has heard me say it, that when I was far away from Scotland, I determined one day to preach in St. Andrews before I died!

"'Therefore, milords, seeing that God has brought my body to the same place where I was first called—being roughly and unjustly taken away at that time, don't stop me from presenting myself to my Brethren tomorrow! As for the danger, rest assured no danger will come to me. My life is in the custody of him whose glory I seek and I can't stop from doing my duty when he makes the way. I don't want any weapons defending me. I demand only an audience, which, if I don't have here at this time, I'll go where I will!'"

Gavin swung around to face Robin and Margaret. "You should have heard him!" The look of triumph glazed his animated face in the telling of the incident. "The room was silent as a tomb after that declaration. Even breathing seemed loud."

"What answer was given to that?" asked Robin.

"Aha! What else but assent! He will preach tomorrow and we will be there," Gavin promised. "Nothing short of death itself will stop us!"

Sunday dawned clear and bright, the sun shining down on St. Andrews Cathedral and on the nobles and their households—along with Margaret and Robin—filing into that massive stone edifice facing toward the North Sea.

Margaret watched John Knox climb fearlessly to the oak pulpit and, with an air of profound authority, open his mouth to preach from the Gospels of Matthew and John concerning the buyers and sellers in the Jerusalem Temple. She heard him liken the ungodly dealings and abominable corruption to the pro-French clergy of this day.

The day following, Knox again gave full exhortation. He preached with wild, energetic fervor. His voice rolled and matched the gestures of his arms, for he spoke with triumph storming in his soul.

Margaret watched the audience of common people, along with bailies and magistrates, go forward to storm the town of all images then light a faggot to the heap. From where Margaret stood with Robin, they gazed at the leaping flames consuming the images at the exact place where Walter Miln had been burned at the stake just one year before.

"Though it won't bring Walter back to life," Robin reflected, "it helps, in part, to repay the injustices of a needless death of a just and godly man."

chapter
20

MARGARET WAS RESTLESS and weary. When the nobles received word that the Regent's troops were heading for Falkland, eighteen miles away, hopes of their own return trip to Edinburgh the following day were snatched away.

If only I could go home. "Home," Margaret smiled knowingly as she whispered the word. "I consider Lord Carlton's home mine." The idea of being Gavin's wife had woven its threads through her mind, dominating her musings. She must put a stop to it.

Robin listened with alarm to the news about the approaching French troops. "We have so few men here," Robin voiced his concern to Gavin, "that if the Regent's troops march against us—and she may order them to do so after the St. Johnston incident—will we be able to get help quickly?"

"Word has already been sent out about the approaching troops," Lord Ballender answered the query with confidence. "We'll be prepared, yes."

Margaret shuddered. Her close brush with death in St. Johnston, still vivid in her mind, was not an occurence she relished having repeated. She would feel safe in Edinburgh, but she knew, if she were there, she would wonder constantly about Robin's and Gavin's safety.

The following day, with news that the Regent's troops were remaining stationary, Robin and Margaret accompanied Lord

Ballender to the house where the nobles met with Knox to discuss their situation.

While Gavin strove behind closed doors, Margaret and Robin walked to the windswept ragged shoreline of St. Andrews to look out over the heaving North Sea. Savage waves rose and fell, venting their fury and gliding silently back into the sea. Gulls squealed overhead, their raucous cries drowning out the sound of Lord Ballender's approach.

"Robin." Gavin's terse words shattered the seaside musings. "Bring Margaret back to the house as soon as possible." Then he turned his horse about and raced away.

A bustle of activity met Robin and Margaret upon their arrival on the scene. Men scurried to form troops, their helmets put in place, swords and spears made ready.

"Officers have been seen scurrying to Cupar, just ten miles from here," Gavin offered in hasty explanation as he shoved his sword into its scabbard at his side, "and they're getting ready for the Regent's arrival. Get your horse for we leave immediately."

Adjusting his mantle and helmet, he turned to Margaret. "I've sent servants to bring your garments from the inn, for you'll remain at Argyll's house until we return. Promise me you will be careful."

"Yes. I promise, milord."

A shout of command tore apart the bracing air, and as Margaret watched in silence, the men raced from St. Andrews, the sunlight sifting through the haze overhead to clearly outline the troops until lost from view.

The house where she stayed was large, but of plain construction, and faced St. Andrews Cathedral, at an angle, from the opposite side of the cobbled street. The sides touched other houses, of similar appearance, in a row the full length of the wynd until the roadway intersected South Street.

After supper, Margaret again walked down the street to the seacoast a short distance from the house. The harsh wind seemed to whip the restlessness from her body as she watched the savage waves rising in white foam over the yellow sands and crashing against the rocks. The lives of the Reformers were as turbulent as the boisterous sea. Would life ever resume a semblance of calm?

The next two days' news was rumor and speculation—embellished as the stories spread from one mouth to another. Imaginative powers were rife.

Eight interminable days inched by, and Margaret asked God on each and every one for the safety of the Reformers—and particularly for Gavin and Robin. Then the nobles and the soldiers returned to their homes and Lord Ballender and his tailor-turned-preacher were reunited with an anxious Margaret.

"We heard many conflicting reports about the fighting," she told Gavin. "What really happened in Cupar?"

"We're made up of a pack of fools," Gavin lamented when he decided to answer her question. "By nightfall, at least three thousand men were in our camp—as if they had rained from the clouds, I swear it! Then early the next morning the fog was as thick as soup and the French tried to maneuver around us, following the stream. By noon they got their first hard look at the number of men they faced—both men and cannon. The wretched French had not bargained for such opposition, so they called a halt. We sent mediators back and forth.

"They asked for an eight-day truce and our incompetent imbeciles of nobles gave it to them!" he exploded. "All we did was march and countermarch. In the meantime, we decided that we'd rid the town of St. Johnston of the French interlopers who had taken over the houses of the Reformers—after the Regent had given her word that she would not put her soldiers in that town! Anyway, a number of our men met at the gates of St. Johnston and sent in a trumpeter and a herald to the Mercat Cross, ordering the enemy to leave the town at once. They sent word of refusal and that they held the town for the Regent. We moved the cannon into place.

"Three of the vile French vermin came out to plead with us to hold our fire. But we refused. By nightfall, we fired the first volley. The French knew they couldn't hold out without reinforcements, so they surrendered and marched out of the town."

"And the townspeople were rejoicing to see them go, no doubt," injected Margaret, absorbing a portion of Gavin's enthusiasm. Positive reports in favor of the Reformers were of short supply so far.

"Absolutely!" he answered. The tone of his voice rose perceptibly.

The Ballender retinue rode south toward Edinburgh the following morning. By evening, the small procession—headed by Lord Ballender—came into Edinburgh and went directly to Carlton House. Gavin fell into bed and lapsed into a sleep of complete exhaustion until morning.

"So!" boomed Lord Carlton when he found his nephew and Margaret at his table for breakfast. "You've joined with the fools who have done nothing but vandalize and loot and burn since this rascal Knox came back to Scotland! What a pity he wasn't burned along with that fool Miln a year ago. Have you seen what these mobs have done to our Abbey here? They even stoned the windows!"

"And you haven't changed a whit, Uncle. You are as pig-headed as ever!" stormed Gavin with eyes ablaze, the memory of recent French treachery still fresh in his mind. "You understand nothing of the French!"

"Silence!" shouted the old man, his face turning a deep shade of crimson. "I'll not have such talk at my table!"

Gavin rose at once and left the castle in a rage.

Margaret put her spoon down, for the food was dry as sawdust in her mouth, choking her. "Would you please excuse me, milord?" she whispered.

"No, I will not. I want to talk to you." Lord Carlton's nostrils dilated with obvious agitation. He noisily drew in air before he continued with his tirade. "What has that miserable whelp been doing with you?"

"Doing, milord?"

"Yes. Have you permitted him . . . certain liberties?"

"Milord," she answered in a voice clear as glass, yet soft as velvet, "I can answer that he has treated me with utmost respect."

166

The old man sat silent as stone with his eyes boring into her lovely face. When she rose, Margaret put her hand gently on his arm and lovingly admitted, "Sir, I am happy to be back. I missed you and am glad to see you looking so well."

Lord Carlton gave a long, deep sigh. "You are the only sane one left, Margaret. If you would just marry that young fool of mine, I could die in peace. Don't you understand, my dear, that I am a very rich man? I would leave everything to you, for you are the only one who can tame him."

"And *you* must understand," Margaret pointed out, "that I am bound by a promise—my sacred word."

"Bah! No, I can't understand it. You have not seen this Corleal in more than a year. How do you know he hasn't married someone else or forgotten you?"

"I don't know, and it may well be that he has. But until the time that I am sure, I remain committed to him."

He closed his eyes a moment, drawing his lips tightly together in agitation. "You English. I can't understand you at all."

When Gavin and Robin returned to the house late that night, they found Margaret sitting before the dying embers of the kitchen fire. She rose immediately and began preparing some mulled ale while they took their places at the small table.

After they had consumed the hot drink, Robin excused himself. But Gavin seemed full of conversation. Margaret reasoned her purpose in remaining with him was an attempt to be of some comfort.

"The Regent is at her crafty worst and screaming we want to kill her," Gavin told her, disgust coating his bristling words. We seized the cunzie stamps this morning to stop her minting inferior coins and causing prices to rise. Now she's raging we went above her authority in doing it. We could do nothing else!" he fumed, furiously flicking a small speck from the table.

"I'm weary, Margaret, but I am pleased to be here—to see you. You have managed to calm my uncle and I'm grateful. I can see he's happy to have you back home."

She smiled at his words, but she did not look up.

"What does he talk about when you're alone?" Gavin placed his large, lean hand on her fingers. "Does he speak of me?"

"At times."

"And about you, too?"

She glanced hastily at the ebony eyes beholding hers, but no response formed on her lips.

"He's right, you know," he pointed out, as though he had read her answer to his question in the look of her eyes. "I need a wife like you, Margaret. That's what he tells you, isn't it?"

"Yes," she admitted. Margaret knew that what he said was too near the truth. She was foolish to stay in the same room with him. Could she ever hope to be happy with Lord Corleal, as his wife? Not one day would pass, as Lady Corleal, that she would not think of this dashing nobleman and wonder with whom he was spending the time—and with whom he was sharing the thrill of his kisses. But no matter, her promise was sure. She would abide by it and trust God and his plan for her life.

chapter
21

EARLY THE NEXT MORNING, before breakfast, Lord Carlton informed Margaret that Henry II of France was dead. "Now that our young queen and her husband are the rightful rulers of Scotland, France, and England, they can settle this fellow Knox and the fools that run after him."

Margaret was thankful that Gavin did not hear that statement from his uncle's lips. Even *she* was upset to think that the feverish efforts of the Reformers might come to naught at the hands of those youthful French rulers.

"Henry tried his best to rid France of those rebellious fanatics, the Huguenots, and vowed to burn their leader, du Bourg, if he ever caught him. And I wish he had! Now with a firm hand from France, we'll have no more of this stealing and burning of kirks and abbeys. Let the Regent burn Knox if she catches him," he growled. "I'll help her."

"Some, milord, feel that speaking against injustices of a clergy that burns men for their faith, and a France that is trying to invade Scotland, is not wrong."

"By thunder," he hurled savagely, "that nephew of mine has you believing it, too!"

"Please, sir," she pleaded softly, "let's talk of other things, for you are upset. Let God take care of these things." Then rising quickly she urged, "Come. Let's take a walk outside while breakfast is being prepared. It's a lovely morning and your plums are growing large. Don't you want to see them?"

"Ah, my dear, I am happy to have you back," he admitted tenderly, his wrath disappearing as suddenly as it had begun.

Margaret smiled, took his arm, and walked with the old man down the forestairs and out into the orchard.

After breakfast, Margaret saw Gavin search the sky before he turned to her with his announcement. "This morning we're going for a ride."

"But I have work to do," she objected immediately, fully aware of his reasons for wanting to ride—the frustration of interminable waiting for the Regent's eight-day truce, added to the aggravation of the stormy differences with his uncle.

"Nonsense. Whatever you have to do can wait. Now get your cloak and I'll order the horses brought to the front of the house."

He gave her no choice. As her place in the house dictated, Margaret was obliged to obey. He helped her onto her mount, and they raced through the wynds to the open spaces beyond the walls of Edinburgh. Together they urged their steeds into the fields of Leith.

"The atmosphere in the house was oppressive," Gavin told Margaret. "If I'd come face to face with my uncle, I'd have exploded, so bear with me and we'll have a little badly needed relaxation and change of scenery." Then tossing a glance Margaret's way he added, "Besides, I want you to meet someone."

Margaret shot him a quizzical look, but he made no further explanation.

They skirted the rugged Calton crags and maneuvered their horses beyond the ripening fields of grain and flocks of sheep, to a rise—some distance away—where they got a perfect view of the city.

"Is there a city anywhere that is located as this one on such a magnificent summit?" Gavin asked, pride swelling within him as he reflected on the regal beauty of the Edinburgh Castle.

"I have heard it likened to Athens, in Greece, but having never seen that city, I consider it hearsay only."

"Come here," Lord Ballender insisted, jumping from his saddle. "Let the horses graze while we sit for a short while. Then we'll move on."

He spanned Margaret's small waist in his hands to help her to the ground. For just an instant, Gavin imprisoned her against her steed and looked into the wind-grazed pink of her cheeks and blue of her eyes. His handsome face was serious, his eyes like firebrands.

Margaret dared not trust herself to return the gaze longer than a fleeting moment. Before she could avoid the inevitable, he pressed his lips to hers and she felt his muscular arms encircling her petite frame with the desire of an ardent lover. She attempted to pull away, but he held her there until she ceased her struggling to be loosed and he could bury his face in her soft golden hair.

"Milord, please, let's move on," she murmured into his shoulder.

Gavin reached up and gently tugged away the strands of windswept hair from her eyes. "How would you react to me if you didn't have the feeble excuse that you are promised to old Corleal?" he challenged suddenly. "Come. Tell me that."

"I can't—when it's not the case."

"Would you want to comfort me when I was weary?"

Margaret moved away from his reach before answering his question. "I suspect you have no lack of comforting arms, milord." She turned and purposely studied the barren hills toward the bay of Leith. A sailing ship made its way slowly toward the open sea, but her mind wasn't fully attuned to the movement. Unconsciously, Margaret's limbs trembled in reaction to Gavin's words.

"Are you jealous, my love?" he grinned, a taunting sparkle dotting each eye.

"Let's get on our way to wherever you are taking me," Margaret urged, "I have to return to the castle before long."

Deftly changing the subject, Gavin pointed out, "Look, Margaret, how high the castle sits on the crag."

She studied the location of the fortress a moment, then made a comment about the news that the old lord had given her earlier. "What will King Henry's death mean to Scotland?"

"First of all," Gavin pointed out, "our Regent is of the French House of Guise. Her daughter, Mary, now the wife of the new king, Francis II, has proclaimed the title of Queen of England, which may well be to our favor and her doom."

"How is that, milord?" Margaret already knew the answer to her question, but her reference kept the subject away from a more personal matter, one that had all the potential for being dangerous.

"Your Queen Elizabeth will not judge this treasonable act lightly. Mary considers Elizabeth a bastard daughter to Henry VIII, and, on that basis—and in the eyes of Catholic France—believes she has the right to the English throne."

"But England . . ."

"In the eyes of Elizabeth or Protestant England, Mary can do nothing. But this may be just the wedge we need to get the new queen's help in our cause. She can use the excuse that she helps us against a foreigner who brazenly alleges a false claim to her crown."

"Why will the Scottish Parliament not judge the matters and claims of the Reformers against the Regent? Surely that would ease the problems."

"Simply because ours is a religious matter and the Parliament will not judge religious matters. Their hands are tied and the Regent knows it. Only the clergy can judge our cause—and you know what their answer would be. But enough of that," he insisted. "Let's move on."

They rode with the wind brushing their faces. Margaret unconsciously thought of another ride—Gavin and Betty Stanus, racing beyond Ballender with the young woman's black hair blowing in the breezes. She recalled Betty's boastful words uttered in St. Giles Kirk. What would Gavin say if she suddenly asked him about the claims Betty had made to her that day?

Margaret followed Lord Ballender for miles along a rural pathway that she recognized as the same route the Reformers, with

Knox in the lead, had taken in May. The horses followed the road westward until they came, suddenly, upon a wall of stone with a huge iron gateway.

Gavin leaped from his horse and called out, "Hello! Are you there?" His hand reached out, yanking a bell unmercifully as an old bent man pushed his head through the open window of a cottage beyond the wall.

"Is it really you, Master Gavin?" he cried out, hurrying to swing open the gate.

"Yes, I have returned! Is Lady Penrith at the castle?"

"Aye, Master, she is and she'll be happy enough to see you!"

A country lane wound its way from the small cottage inside the wall gate, past grazing cattle and a deep and broad quarry hole, coming at last to a stone castle rising five stories into the air.

Gavin led Margaret to the back of the mansion where a door opened into a round stairwell. But before he could enter so much as his foot inside the doorway a voice called out, "Gavin Ballender. Is that you?"

"None other, Aunt Sophia!"

The old woman hurried toward the house on the arm of her maid and looked upon her handsome nephew with a glint of love spilling from those same black eyes Margaret now knew as a family trait. "So you have not forgotten me, after all." Then turning to face Margaret she said, "and this is your wife, no doubt, that I've heard nothing about?"

"She's not my wife yet, Aunt, but she will be." Gavin glanced at Margaret and when she turned crimson as a blooming rhododendron, smiling not at all, he just put his arm possessively about her shoulders and laughed.

"Ah, yes, you always commanded the eyes of the ladies." Then with an impatient wag of her hand she nodded toward the doorway. "But come inside, my dears, and have a bite of food with me. You must be hungry after your long ride."

Margaret was seething with indignation at the blatant audacity of

Lord Ballender in making such a claim before the world, but she would not appear a beast of a guest to so amiable a hostess as Aunt Sophia. Not yet, at least.

The flustered little maid was hurriedly sent on to the kitchen to relay the message to the cook that refreshments were to be sent immediately to the guests in the hall.

The large room to which Gavin's aunt took them occupied the whole floor of the castle as, obviously, did rooms on each floor above it and below.

"Do sit down," invited Lady Penrith.

Gavin took the seat next to his aunt. Margaret sat opposite in a high-backed chair. All the seats formed a semi-circle about the fireplace.

While the two chatted, Margaret studied the timbered and paneled room. The walls were thick with deep-set windows looking out over the quarry hole and an old gnarled chestnut tree.

"So, dear Gavin, you are taking a wife at last." Lady Penrith's eyes lighted on the girl sitting in stoney silence opposite. "Your Uncle Edmund is happy now, isn't he, with so bonny a bride? He was very adamant about leaving his fortune to a wife of his choosing. Isn't he pleased?"

Without a flicker in Gavin's eye he spun out the reply. "He couldn't be more pleased."

"When is the wedding? I am invited, aren't I?"

"Of course! The date is unsure, but then we will certainly inform you." At Margaret's angry glance he added, "I want to show Margaret the Firth from the back lawn. It's been a favorite view of mine since I was a boy." Gavin rose and patted his aunt's arm. "We will take but a few minutes."

Margaret smiled pleasantly at the woman as long as she was in view, but when she and Gavin were well beyond the house and out of hearing she demanded, "Why did you lie to your aunt?"

"Lie?" The lord's reply was indignant, accompanied with a glint of amusement and a laugh. "I most certainly didn't lie. I asked you to marry me, didn't I?"

"But I didn't consent to any such thing—nor do I intend to."

"Don't be too sure of that, my love."

"I will not marry anyone simply to save an inheritance."

"What made you think my inheritance had anything to do with my wanting to marry you?"

"Your uncle, for one." She really did not wish to mention Betty Stanus and their conversation.

"There must have been another," Gavin bit out. "Who?"

chapter
22

THE FOLLOWING MORNING Gavin left with a representative group for Dunbar Castle to meet with the Regent. Margaret heard his horse's hoofs clattering from the cow-bil along the street.

Robin and she donned their cloaks to walk to Holyrood Palace and Abbey. From the cobbled street, they viewed silently the wreckage the Reformers had wrought in their anger and frustration. Where high Gothic windows had formerly arched skyward, now empty spaces allowed the light of day to show through to the floor. Not a door or a window was intact. No ornament nor image could be found. A shell of barren, fire-blackened wall was a monument to the hatred that burned in the Scottish hearts against injustices.

"How long can this possibly go on?" Margaret asked, dismayed at the havoc.

"As long as it takes to rid the realm of French domination. The common people have no other recourse in venting their protests." Robin's words held no hint of compromise.

Slowly they retraced their steps up High Street to amble through the Canongate area, past the old and gloomy Tolbooth and the stone houses with roofs of thatched heather. A few tradesmen chatted. Others argued.

The sky was gray and smelled of rain. Robin and Margaret walked on past the Luckenbooths by St. Giles Kirk and the Mercat Cross. Coarsely dressed townsmen bought and merchants sold as if the past days' deeds were mere trivialities.

They came to the crest of the Castle Hill, and Margaret noted that the walls connected square towers while the castle itself hugged the rock with its treacherous, dizzying drop to the loch below.

"What will the nobles discuss with the Regent at Dunbar Castle?" Margaret asked, breaking the silence of their walk.

"They will offer obedience for religious freedom," explained Robin. "And they will also ask that the ignorant, unlearned clergy be removed from the kirks along with the French troops from the country."

"Then the requests have not changed."

"Not a whit."

By evening Lord Ballender dropped into a seat in the kitchen, weary and angry. "We accomplished nothing with the obstinate woman." His teeth ground in frustration. "But then, I expected nothing else."

"Did she give in on any of the issues at all?" asked Robin.

"Of course not. She pretended to accept religious freedom—with conditions, of course—and flatly refused to get rid of the incompetent clergy or to send the French troops packing." His words were coated with bitterness.

"But you *did* try. She can never deny your attempt at reasoning."

"She can—and does—say any damnable thing she pleases. She *will* flatly deny our efforts of this day." A loud exhaling of breath followed.

"What happens now?" Robin asked.

"We sit and wait—we'll rot waiting." Gavin rose from his seat and paced. "We could, Robin, have taken the French at Cupar, but we didn't. What a travesty!" he stormed. "This whole sorry mess could be over and done with by now if we had. Instead, here we are. We're weak—cursedly so. The Brethren left for their homes when they heard the Regent had left Edinburgh. We don't have wealthy men on our side to back us, and we lack regular troops. So we can't use what we have, for they aren't prepared in ways of fighting to the point of being effective."

Closing his eyes a moment and leaning against the fireplace

beams, Gavin vented his inner seething. "If *only*—if *only* we had taken the enemy when we had the golden opportunity at Cupar!"

Robin broke Gavin's bitter reflections. "We need England's help badly, I see."

"If we don't get it, our cause is doomed."

"How does Mr. Knox feel about that?"

"He realizes we're desperate for men and money. If only our representatives to the English Court could persuade Elizabeth to help us act quickly. We could make a hasty end to all this if we just acted *now*. Why is Elizabeth so thick-headed as to not see that? What's it going to take for her to finally do something?"

Margaret listened to all of the conversation silently while she sliced bread and meat for supper. Outside, the rain blew hard against the windows. It seemed to moan in sympathy to Gavin. The accompanying gloom of the room and its occupants matched the dismal dampness of the outside. Every movement was shadowed— as a mime—on the wall opposite, illuminated by the small lamp burning bravely on the table.

Finally Robin advised, "We must pray about it, milord. God knows the hopelessness of our situation. He is not looking for strength of numbers but for willing and obedient hearts. Remember Gideon and the lapping soldiers?" he offered with encouragement.

Gavin took a huge bite of meat and sighed dispiritedly. "I hope you're right. For *all* our sakes."

Lord Carlton kept William and Margaret busy from sunup to sundown with remedies for this ache and that. "Blasted foul weather, this," he complained. "For one month—June—I feel good, and then it ends. The chill cold from the sea is unhealthy; I'm convinced of it." The man leaned back in his chair and pursed his lips. "You must go back to Ballender, Margaret, for your health."

Margaret sighed. She gave up arguing about the fact that she had no intention of living there—nor could she even if she wanted to.

For a few moments she considered the old man's comments. How happy she could be if the situation were altered. If she had

179

never known the Lord of Corleal, and Lord Ballender wanted her for his wife simply because he loved her—not because of an inheritance—if she claimed Gavin's whole attention and affections, and he had the peace of God in his soul, as she did, she could be truly happy.

Before she gave herself too far over to the foolish abandonment of dreaming, Margaret brought herself firmly back to reality. She was a promised woman. That unalterable truth did not give a great amount of comfort, but it did keep her head straight.

Gavin and Robin took Margaret with them to Lord Auchler's mansion by the Canongate arch for a meeting. When John Knox came into the room, he noticed her at once and smiled one of his rare pleasantries, adding a kind word. "Miss Chilton, I believe."

She nodded. When the man smiled, the fullness of his ruddy cheeks pushed his eyes into even deeper hollows. But the sternness of his face softened for only a moment before he abruptly moved on. His coarse doublet had shirred sleeves, but no frill, no pretention toward fashion. He went immediately to the head of the table and became a firm authority to the Brethren.

"Milords," he began sternly, "our situation is perilous. We need the backing of money and we need regular troops, neither of which we have—or are likely to have unless God undertakes to supply that need. The Regent has Huntly to fight for her in the north, McConnell in the west, Kennedies in the south. We have Hepburn and Bothwell to deal with in the Lothian area."

His look was stern but not harsh. When he ended his speech—with a plea for prayer—a hum of discussion followed and dragged on into the afternoon. The cause for freedom was in serious trouble unless God intervened to supply a willing Elizabeth to help them.

Two days later, Gavin sped to the house and found Margaret tidying the hall as his unlcle sat in his chair by the fire.

"Margaret, I wish to speak to you," he urged.

"Speak then," Lord Carlton bellowed, "for she won't leave this room until I permit it!"

"Very well, Uncle, I will inform you both. The French plan to march into Edinburgh and I want to move both of you away from this house to Aunt Sophia's before they swarm in."

"I say no," the old man answered instantly.

"If anything happens to Margaret, Uncle," he vowed with venom lacing his clipped words, "I will hold you responsible!" His voice rose to a shout. "The French soldiers are swine and have no respect for our women!"

"You will remember that I am a loyal subject of the Regent and they will not come near this house!" thundered his uncle in return, rising to his feet and pointing his cane accusingly. "It's your fault— along with these idiots you hang about with—who brought us to this impasse. Now get out!"

"Margaret," Gavin pleaded, searching her face, "please be cautious. I'll leave two of my soldiers to guard you. Now come and at least see me off!"

She accompanied him as far as his stallion and waited for him to prepare to race off. "There will be trouble," he warned with a tightening of lips. "We don't have the men to face the French army yet. We're going to seize Stirling Castle, but it's impossible to get word to our men in the west, for the attack is coming on us too suddenly. I told them to prepare but they wouldn't listen!"

Gavin slammed his helmet on his head and adjusted his musket and sword. He placed his hands on Margaret's shoulders, disregarding the crimson hue of embarrassment that overtook her, and her unsuccessful attempt to pull back. "Knox has gone to meet with the English. Pray he accomplishes something for our cause. Willock has taken over as preacher of St. Giles, so if you need help, go to him— but take one of the soldiers I'm leaving behind."

"I understand."

Then kissing her hastily before she could move back, he leaped onto the saddle and motioned for Robin and the two remaining soldiers to follow.

With a sinking heart, Margaret watched them ride away. "God," she whispered desperately, "keep them safe."

Near the end of July, word reached Margaret that three thousand French troops had marched on Leith. With no shot fired, the gates were opened to them and the helpless Reformers rushed in vain to overtake them before they entrenched firmly in the fortified seaport town.

The Reformers, stationing themselves outside the city gates of Edinburgh, and maneuvering from the east, stood their ground and refused the enemy entrance into the town of Edinburgh as well.

"A truce was made at the quarry holes near Leith." Gavin sighed dispiritedly after making his alarming announcement. "Some of our Reformers signed the truce without the rest of us present. The French soldiers are taking over our men's homes, eating their food and abusing the families unmercifully. One man in Leith resisted the wretches and they killed him!" Gavin stormed, his voice rising to fever pitch with the telling.

On Sunday, as Willock preached, Margaret was stunned to see French captains and their soldiers strolling through the kirk, talking in loud voices so the people couldn't hear the preaching. Back and forth they paraded in full view until Willock cried out, "O God! Rid us of these locusts who have come in amongst us!"

Before she realized that she had done so, Margaret reached over and laid her hand gently on Gavin's, feeling the murderous tension in his fingers as he handled the musket, fiercely holding back a savagely lethal desire to kill. Willock exhorted the Reformers to remain calm and not break the truce. "Be above this thing!" he urged. "God will deliver us in his own time!"

October brought with it cold, damp days, increasingly dark mornings, and early nightfalls. The Reformers defiantly held Edinburgh and announced at the Mercat Cross that they no longer recognized the Regent as their ruler, demanding that the French leave Leith within twenty-four hours. The crowds murmured and spilled out anger and rumbling invectives against the injustices they suffered.

"We have a spy among us," Gavin related wearily that night as he paced before the fire. "If I ever find out who he is, I'll personally hang the worm! Not only that, our cunzie stamps were stolen. We have no money. In one of the skirmishes outside Edinburgh, the Earl of Argyll's son was killed by the French swine. If it had been my son that was killed," he vowed with unswerving hatred, "I would have stormed with murder in my eyes and killed every enemy soldier I came to! But he acted with amazing calm."

"Faith, milord, is the answer," Margaret answered softly but firmly. "It works miracles."

On Sunday, Knox preached with great power, using the eightieth Psalm as his text. After the service, the nobles tarried and Margaret sat in the shadow of a great stone pillar near the North Porch to wait and listen. "Have you heard?" Lord Auchler asked Gavin softly, "England is sending us money in the amount of four thousand crowns. Ormiston has ridden to Berwick to get it."

"Ah," Lord Ballender agreed, "that's good news. And what about the rumor of the Regent's secretary?"

Margaret studied the handsome man with his fitted hose and crimson doublet as he spoke to Auchler. He stood with feet apart and hands folded behind him. His eyes sparkled with a fresh enthusiasm at the news and he grinned with pleasure when Lord Auchler said, "It's no rumor. Last night he escaped from the French guards at the Leith gates and surrendered himself to us at once."

"Has the Regent any nobles left with her at all?"

"Just a few clergy—the rest are all French soldiers."

"With not a drop of loyalty except the pay they draw."

chapter

23

Word reached the Reformers that Ormiston had been captured and beaten, and the desperately needed four thousand crowns had been stolen. A doleful gathering of nobles congregated at the kirk for a few moments of preaching, with muskets and swords in readiness. The air outside was as wet and foul as the mood within the church building. Only Robin and John Knox remained undaunted, and even Margaret felt hurt and discouraged.

Knox climbed the few steps to his plain wooden pulpit and preached a short but vehement message, touching on the sins that so easily beset them and the great hope that rests in placing one's life wholly in God's care and strength. He had barely concluded when a muffled noise reached the ears of those sitting and standing in the kirk.

The noblemen snatched their muskets, donned their helmets, raced out through the North Porch of St. Giles to their horses, and were gone from sight. The other worshippers, in hot pursuit, sought to learn what the increasing din could mean.

High Street was filled with soldiers of Edinburgh and of Dundee, running in the direction of the kirk, and the air was rent with screams of terror. Men, women, and children scattered like dry leaves before a windstorm.

A voice rang out: "The whole French army comes in from Leith Wynd Gate!" Soldiers turned to escape through Nether Bow Port as others tried desperately to enter. Hordes of citizens tried in vain to escape through the guarded West Gate. A great cry arose, followed by a sudden explosion of cannon from Edinburgh Castle. Fresh screams of terror rang throughout the town.

Above the houses, a thick column of smoke rose from the direction of Canongate where thatched roofs took fire from the cannon balls. As Margaret and Robin looked on in horror, French horsemen pursued the retreating Reformers, their swords wielding deadly and merciless vengeance on every man, woman, and child standing in the way.

And then, almost as quickly as it had begun, the racing ceased. The sounds that remained were not of soldiers and horses' hoofs striking the worn stone pavement, but the wails and sobs of the victims.

Few that convened the following morning in St. Giles kirk, with swords at their sides and muskets in hand, were untouched by the miseries and heartaches of the previous day. Their faces mirrored the penetrating chill and dampness of the kirk as they sought the warm encouragement they knew only the Word of God could give. After the service they drew together, seeking additional information on the happenings of the previous day.

"The men from Dundee," Gavin expounded, his teeth grinding in anger, "took artillery and hackbuts and dragged them up the crags toward Leith. All would have gone well if they could have done it secretly. But something went wrong. A traitor from our forces in Edinburgh sent word to the enemy—before our reinforcements arrived—that the Dundee men were there, as ducks in a marsh. The swine swarmed out of Leith and attacked. Dundee resisted for a while but the cowards who called themselves soldiers—the ones who were supposed to help him—fled. The Dundee men couldn't hold. The trained French pursued them into Edinburgh with our captured artillery!"

"What of the report that the whole French army was coming in from Leith Wynd?" demanded Auchler.

"An enemy trick. After that it was disaster. Our soldiers were absolutely worthless. They have had no training against such trained French warfare and knocked each other over at Nether Bow Gate," Gavin admitted sadly. "We have nothing but volunteers against an army that is highly trained."

"But you must admit that some of the nobles gathered round and took swift action to save our artillery, charging in hot pursuit to draw the wretches away from Edinburgh."

"Yes," added Gavin bitterly, "after the French killed women and children."

Margaret rose quickly to still the nausea rising in her stomach. She put her hands to her face. "O God," she whispered, "undertake to help us."

"Is my nephew in the house?" Lord Carlton asked the following morning at his breakfast.

"No, milord. He left after breakfast," answered Margaret.

"Well, at last he learned another hard lesson, didn't he? Eh? He will learn to interfere with our Regent and speak disrespectfully." The old man stuffed the last of his bread into his mouth and shook a finger at Margaret. "Didn't I warn him against this heretic, Knox? The lot of them will be shown for what fools they are. I understand one of the Regent's men intercepted a heretic carrying four thousand crowns—money from England."

Lord Carlton leaned back with a look of smug satisfaction creasing his face. He took a long draught of ale. "Four thousand crowns. That will keep the Regent's soldiers in pay for a long, long time."

But what of the core of determined men, paid only with the knowledge that they would possess a pure heart and conscience toward God? Margaret dared not voice her thoughts, for fear she might later regret her words. Lord Carlton had failed to recognize the ungodly behavior of the Regent and her lieges. Certainly they had no love for Scotland.

The food victualers, being sent for the Reformers from London, were expected to arrive sometime the following week. From the third-story window, Margaret looked toward Calton Hill, where the captain of the horsemen searched the Firth daily, waiting impatiently for the first signs of the billowing English sails. Gusts of cold salt air blew in from the Firth. And hanging like a pall above all was the foreboding of doom.

During her periodic trips to the third story in search of movement abroad, Margaret was rewarded with nothing more than the motion of the kites flying in great circles, and the herons dipping to the sedgy pools before rising and flying gracefully away. And then she saw ships sailing into the bay and maneuvering toward the coast near Leith. Her heart raced at the thought of signals being given and the Reformers' horsemen riding forth to meet them.

Her pulse thundered in her temples. "No!" she cried out. "No, Lord!" For French horsemen raced from the Leith fort to intercept the Reformers a few moments later. She turned her face away, unable to watch the desperate battle between the Reformers and the well-trained troops that swarmed from the fortress to intercept the supply ship from London.

"Lord," Margaret pleaded, "keep Gavin and Robin safe." How much more could the Reformers take, she wondered, and still survive?

Time seemed unendurable. Hours dragged as days. When the frantic knock sounded at the door, Margaret's heart froze within her. Somehow, even before William answered and rushed to relay the news, she knew that the messenger bore tragic tidings. Unconsciously, Margaret hurried up the steps from the kitchen as William rushed in to inform old Lord Carlton of the news.

"Milord, Lord Ballender and Robin have been wounded. Margaret is urged to bring supplies as soon as possible. One of the soldiers from Ballender is waiting at the door."

Her hands trembled as she rushed to get her cloak and a few things to take with her. Lord Carlton stood as silent as stone after he heard the news. William led him back into the hall and to a chair.

"Rest, milord," Margaret encouraged Lord Carlton as she prepared to take her leave, "and we will bring them both here as soon as possible. All will be well." She spoke softly, desperately trying to assure him, as well as herself, of the truth of the words she spoke. The old man merely nodded without looking up from the fire. Margaret dashed through the doorway and down the forestairs of the house.

The soldier helped Margaret onto his horse and they rode frantically through the streets of Edinburgh to a Canongate inn where some of the seriously wounded lay. Her eyes scanned the grisly scene of men who had hastily been placed side by side on the wooden floor to bear their pain as best they could. The Ballender soldier took Margaret directly to a corner where Gavin, his doublet soaked with blood, held Robin in his arms.

"I don't doubt God's mercy," Robin said aloud, "for it was purchased by the blood of Jesus Christ." He paused and closed his eyes a moment before continuing. "I am not sorry that it pleased God to make me worthy to shed blood for his cause, for I am ready to meet him." Again he took a weak breath and looked up into Gavin's eyes. "I do not regret spending my days in so just a cause."

Margaret knelt silently, placing her hands over her mouth as tears burst unchecked down her face and dropped onto her cloak. "No," she whispered desperately, "not Robin, Lord. Do not take him from me." Her words choked in her throat as she sobbed amidst the rising, agonizing cries of the wounded lying all about her.

When Robin's head fell to the side, Gavin placed him gently onto the floor and knelt beside him to mutter inaudible words in his grief. When Lord Ballender finally rose, he staggered unsteadily, and would have fallen had Margaret not steadied his balance. He clasped his arms about her and wept uncontrollably for Robin and the miserable, heartbreaking setback the Reformers had been again dealt that day.

"Come," she pleaded, "let's go home."

Arriving at the mansion, after an agonizing journey by horseback, Gavin let Margaret help him into bed, wincing with pain, sweat breaking out in beads across his brow. Tenderly, Margaret removed his torn and blood-soaked doublet so she could sponge his shattered arm with warm water, the raw flesh hanging in loose pockets. As she did so, he slipped into unconsciousness.

Forcing back the drops that misted her eyes, Margaret ripped a linen cloth into strips and wrapped the bands about his arm before pulling the blankets over his limp body. Then, kneeling at his side, she placed her hand gently on his injured arm and prayed as the tears spilled onto his covering. "Spare his life, Lord," she begged. "I couldn't stand to lose him, too. He—he means so much to me."

By evening, Gavin opened his eyes and saw Margaret sitting by his bed, anxiously watching over him. "Can you drink a little broth, milord?" she whispered, placing a cool hand on his one good arm.

"A little, yes."

Margaret rose and went to the fireplace where she had kept a kettle warm in case he woke and was hungry. She ladled a little of the liquid into a cup. Taking a spoon, she blew it cool and placed her hand gently under his head to help him drink.

"The French wounded one of our leaders and when they recognized him, they kept wounding him until he died," related Gavin, the tears running down his face as he told it. "But the man's heart was right before God and he didn't turn and rail against his persecutors. And Robin—"

"Hush, " she whispered, placing the cup aside and brushing back the matted hair from his forehead. "What is done is done. We go on," she encouraged, her voice thick with grief as her hand lay gently on his chest.

"I asked God to give me the kind of faith that you and those two had, Margaret. It was strange. I felt great warmth surrounding me. And now I have a completely different reason for fighting. Before it was political. Now, for me, it is wholly the cause of freedom to worship God as I please."

Margaret began to cry silently as she listened to the words he spoke. Her fingers clasped the lord's hand tightly and she smiled. "Then he has answered."

He put his arm out to Margaret and pulled her face down to his shoulders. "I love you," he whispered. "I can't help it." She felt the dampness of her eyes soak the covering, but she couldn't pull away. "I will do my best to keep you from going to Corleal," he promised, "for I can't lose you, Margaret."

While she placed a bed of heather on the floor near the fireplace in Gavin's chamber—to be close by in case he needed something during the night—she could only think of his words, words that declared the love that she had fought against for so many long months.

For an endless time she stared into the fire, seeing nothing but his eyes in the intense flame. Margaret thought of the handsome set of his jaw—the slight curl of black hair falling over his brow in disarray in the shadows of his room. And her heart swelled over his confession of his faith in God.

And Robin—how happy he would be knowing that his testimony and death had served its purpose. Gavin was now, also, ready to meet God. So merciful a Father must also see her own plight. As the tears slipped from the corners of her eyes and spilled onto the sheet under her, Margaret knew that one immutable fact remained—she must remain true to her word of promise to Lord Corleal. No doubt he would come looking for her. But she remained unsure of how he would be affected by her captivity; perhaps he would vent his revenge on Lord Ballender.

The tears continued to flow. The fire burned low and when the gentle tapping of the rain increased to a sharp staccato, she turned her face heavenward.

"O Lord," she pleaded under her breath, her head gently rocking back and forth, "only you have the power to take these coming weeks of hopelessness facing not only me, but all the Reformers, and turn them to your good. Keep us all under the protection of your great love."

chapter

24

THE FOLLOWING DAY was clear but cold. Margaret placed another blanket on Gavin, then added more fuel to the fire to drive the encroaching chill from the room.

The doctor arrived about midmorning, and grimly, silently removed the dressing Margaret had applied. "Your wound is clean," he told Gavin, "and should heal well if the dressing is changed often. But you will be unable to travel for a while. That spear did a thorough job on your arm."

"What is the situation since yesterday?" Gavin asked, searching the man's face.

The surgeon sighed. "Not good." He shook his head sadly and looked down at his hands. "The Reformers evacuated after much debating by the leaders at the Tolbooth until late last night. Some wanted to stay and hold out but they were outvoted. Knox departed to Stirling with the remaining soldiers, under the vile insults and stones hurled at them by the citizens."

"Then I must get there, too," Gavin insisted, trying to rise.

"You'll go nowhere, milord," the doctor warned, forcing him back onto the bed. "You would be no more than an unneeded burden." The man released his breath slowly and rose. "You'll get back in time. Just be patient. I am afraid the worst is yet to come."

After the doctor had taken his leave, Gavin turned to Margaret. "I would never have believed our people would turn on us. Knox must be heartbroken."

"But not for long, Gavin," she admitted. "Not if I know the character of the man. He is grief-stricken now, but his faith will rally and surmount this, too."

Lord Carlton hobbled to the second story and into his nephew's room. Margaret held her breath, in fear of a violent outbreak of temper, and in the the darkness of a black and brooding morning, she knelt to stir the fire in order to relieve her tension.

"Your arm is healing, is it?" asked the old man, a touch of concern permeating his words.

"Yes, Uncle. But then, I have the best of care."

"Umm," he grunted. Lord Carlton looked about, then seated himself in the chair by the bed. "You aren't going to be foolish enough to leave before it's completely healed, are you?"

"No. I'm at your mercy until then. I've found I'm no match for a javelin or a hackbut."

"Give up this foolish business now that you are wounded. Settle down. Be a respectable gentleman—marry and have a family."

"That time is not yet upon me."

"Then you will get yourself killed," the old man said with rising irritation and a solid thump of his cane on the floor.

Gavin smiled. "When God is foremost in your life," he answered softly but firmly, "he is worth dying for. If God wills, I am, like Robin, ready to die for him. I have, through all this, come to know God, and my life is now his. It took this blow to bring me to the realization that my life was not what it should or could have been. But now I know I can follow no other course."

Lord Carlton drew in his breath and lifted his bearded chin before he rose and thumped his way out of the room. "That is heresy and you're a fool," he grumbled. "A plain fool."

December was raw and wet when the Lords Ballender and Auchler left the gates of Edinburgh behind and rode off toward Stirling Castle, uncertain of what lay ahead for the Reformers. Margaret watched them disappear in the distance, and turned to place her cloak about her shoulders. *Go with them, Lord,* she breathed silently.

When the rain ceased one of the servants accompanied Margaret to the marketplace for supplies. The wind's icy blasts whipped their cloaks and tore at their hair as they hurried to finish their business of buying so they could return home again to the coziness of the fireplace.

But over the whining of the wind, Margaret heard a familiar voice. She turned in its direction and was surprised to see, across the street, Betty Stanus, clinging tightly to a French officer. Margaret studied the pair until they disappeared into one of the narrow closes leading from High Street.

And then the stark realization hit her. Could Betty possibly be the traitor? Margaret's mind whirled with memories—of the angry words of the Reformers when they realized a traitor was in the camp; of Betty's attending the gatherings with her brother-in-law, a town burgess.

Perhaps it is because of me she has fallen traitor—stooped so low as to turn against the Reformers to find revenge against Gavin.

Margaret felt the deep pain of anguish cut through her heart as if a knife had been hurled inside her and twisted unmercifully. She picked up her purchases, drew her cloak tightly about her, and made her way against the raw edge of the frigid blasts back to the mansion.

The days crept along slowly with no word of the Reformers' whereabouts. Margaret grew uneasy. She knew the French would not sit idly by while the Scottish nobility planned with England. Of this, she was sure.

For Lord Carlton's sake, Margaret attempted to be cheerful, but he sank deeper into his own solitude and dejection. "We shall have a plum cake for Yule," Margaret told him when the twenty-third came and passed with no word of his nephew.

"I had not thought I would pass my last days so sadly," the old man whispered. He appeared even older, and his eyes had the doleful look of a hound. "Christmas was always a joyful time when my wife lived. She had so looked forward to the day when the two of us would sit about the fireside with the children of our nephew on our knees. We were not blessed with offspring, but she . . . and I . . . felt the ties of love with Gavin." He twisted the knob of his cane as a tear trickled down his pale cheek.

"You have good years left to you yet; you shall see." Margaret assured him. *If only Gavin would arrive home safely, in time for Yule!*

For a time, the only sounds to be heard were the wind whistling down the chimney and the rain beating against the windows. And then, as Margaret rose to add peat to the fire, she heard another sound, that of someone trying to gain entrance to the main door. She went and opened it cautiously, peering out into the darkness to see—Gavin!

Her eyes lit with pleasure at the sight of him. He threw off his soggy mantle and put his arm about her before he glanced at the old man huddled in his chair.

"Uncle," he nodded. For a fleeting moment, Margaret thought she saw a flicker of pleasure in the man's bearded face before Gavin moved to the fire to warm himself. "It's a miserable night and I'm truly glad to be home."

"You had no business out at all," answered his uncle bitterly.

"I'll get you a hot drink," offered Margaret, jumping up. "You must be chilled to the bone. Is your arm well?" she queried with concern.

"Well enough."

Margaret brought him a hot cup and watched him sip it slowly. Her heartbeat accelerated at the joy of having him near, remembering the days of Gavin's illness.

Lord Carlton sat awhile in silence, then called for William to help him to bed.

"I'm so glad you are safe," she said softly when she was alone with Gavin.

"When we came back into town, we learned that the French troops had missed finding us by but a few hours' time at Stirling."

"The important thing is that they *did* miss you," she offered encouragingly. "The Lord mercifully saw to that."

"True." Gavin pulled a chair closer to the fire and motioned for her to do the same. Glancing into Margaret's face he admitted, "I've really missed you." When he reached over and placed his hand on hers, she felt the warmth throughout her entire body. She couldn't draw it away though she knew it to be wrong.

"We have received word that English ships on the Thames in London are being fitted for war and that Admiral Winter has been assigned the command."

"Then help is on the way."

"Yes. Help is coming. But who knows when it will arrive? We decided at Stirling that each man must fend for himself until help gets here. We have vowed to harrass the enemy at every possible opportunity. Elizabeth promised help when she learned, from Knox, that the French court had adopted arms quartered with the English crest. She was furious! It's out and out treason!"

"So you will be here awhile?"

"Until we see what the French have in mind. They may decide to attack." Gavin turned to the woman beside him as the lazy hooded look of his eyes sent a reaction spearing into the center of her heart. His arm tugged around her shoulders. "Corleal will not have you," he vowed, pulling Margaret to her feet and burying his face in the softness of her hair. "I'm sorry that I did not find you first, for if I had, you would be my wife by now and I would be extremely reluctant to leave you for even a moment."

Margaret wished it, too, although she held her tongue, certain Gavin was aware of the reactions his presence produced.

At the end of January, Gavin rode into Edinburgh with the first good news any of them had heard in months. He found Margaret in the kitchen and sat beside her in front of the fire to relate the events of the past two weeks.

"The French general marched north from Stirling without opposition, feeling the sweet taste of success in his mouth. When he looked out over the firth, he saw what he thought were the sails of the French supply ships coming to his aid. With a haughty salute and much shouting, he shot a volley to let them know he was there on the shore. To the wretch's great shock the sails were English! Aha! Admiral Winters intercepted the supply ships near Leith plus two guard vessels and one artillery supply vessel! With this, French supplies were cut off from France.

"The French general, with practically nothing to eat, returned to Stirling as quickly as he had left it. Nor did the army dare look for food along the way for fear of bitter attacks from the people." The dancing lights of thankfulness twinkled in Gavin's eyes. "Do you see what God has done for us, Margaret?" he beamed.

She looked down suddenly, with her lashes sweeping her cheeks. The pleasure of the news suddenly disappeared from her face as she whispered, "The English nobles will be marching north soon then, won't they?"

"Yes." Studying Margaret's face in the blazing heat from the fire, he pulled her to her feet as he rose. "Do you love me, Margaret?" he demanded.

She chewed at her lower lip a few moments before looking into the ebony depths of his eyes. The wetness in her eyes made his outline a hazy blur. "Please don't ask me that." Gavin's arms folded about her shoulders and he held her close.

As a result of spring rains, Edinburgh turned into an endless lake reflecting the blue of the sky all the way to Leith and the coast bordering the Firth.

Lord Carlton received his friend Anson one afternoon while Margaret sat by the window in the hall, mending sheets.

"From the looks of the area, we can be thankful that we reside on high ground," he commented with a shake of his head. "Water all around us. I'm beginning to understand how Noah must have felt." For a few moments the two men sat quietly before Anson broke the short silence.

"I have been doing some thinking about our situation—yours and mine."

"Oh?" commented Lord Carlton distrustfully, his brows rising with attentiveness for what would follow.

"When we were in Parliament, we had some say in our government. Now we have none. Your nephew knows this and you· and I know it."

"What are you trying to tell me, Anson?" the old man questioned suspiciously. "Speak up! Out with it!"

"Just this. I can no longer stand behind our Regent. The French are merciless. They steal, burn, and kill with her blessing. They are actually taking over the homes of our citizens and pushing them out into the streets."

Lord Carlton looked at his friend through squinting, suspecting eyes as if he prepared to devour the man. "The heretics asked for this—"

"No, they didn't."

"I don't believe it!"

Anson's voice was as unyielding as stone. "It's time we took our heads out of the mud and faced the truth. I've watched Gavin and Auchler. They possess something you and I don't. God is on their side. Did you hear what happened to the proud French fleet heading here from France when the storm hit?"

"Tell me."

"Eighteen of the ensigns drowned even before they left port and when the remainder left, this storm hit. That was not chance, my friend. That was God's doing. Now the Regent is dying. That, too, is ominous, for she rages against her Maker." Anson sighed. "I must know what it is that Knox speaks of—this faith and forgiveness."

Margaret listened, her heart pounding a melody in her chest. She was afraid to breathe for fear it would deter Anson's intent. *O God, she prayed silently, let both of them find you in all your wonderful fullness.*

"I miss the old days," Lord Carlton reminisced again. "They were such good times."

"We were fooled even then."

chapter
25

WHEN WORD OF THE TREATY with England reached the Regent, she turned an unseeing eye on the French soldiers' retaliation. The troops hurled themselves into a reckless fury, smashing mills, mercilessly destroying crops, and, heedless of the pleading owners' cries, driving sheep, oxen, pigs, and horses into the fortified stronghold of Leith.

For days the onslaught continued with furious abandon. In the midst of it, Gavin raced into town. "There is going to be fighting," he warned his uncle, "and I want to take Margaret and you away from here."

"Take Margaret," Lord Carlton said defiantly, "but I will not leave my home."

"The English will arrive tomorrow but I fear the French. They're bent on destruction, sparing no one." Then Gavin hunkered down before his old uncle, looking into his face. "Uncle, I fear for you."

"For my money," the old man snorted.

"Your money be hanged. It's *you* I care about!"

His uncle leaned heavily on his cane, unchecked tears forming in his eyes.

Gavin flung his arms around the old stooped shoulders. "Forgive me," he whispered, as the two embraced and wept.

"My sister's castle contains a hidden room," the old man said softly, when he gained his composure. "If you want to take Margaret there, do it, but I won't step one foot from my home."

"No, milord," she objected immediately. "I can't leave you. Besides," her words softened to a near whisper, "I—I have an appointment to keep." She had heard Gavin's audible admission that an inheritance was of no importance to him. If that were true, then she must believe that he cared for her, too. But the fact still remained that she was a promised woman.

"What makes you cling so savagely to that loyalty of yours? Doesn't love count for anything?" Gavin demanded harshly.

Margaret closed her eyes and the tears squeezed out as she bit her lower lip to quell the aching of her heart. "Please don't torture me," she begged. "If God has other plans for me, they will come to pass."

"Don't you think I've been tortured, too," he insisted, "seeing you day after day, knowing that despite my love for you, you wait for a man you don't love simply because you feel honorbound to a promise that was given almost two years ago?"

"And if you were the man I waited for?"

"If I were Corleal, I would have moved heaven and earth to find you!"

On April second, the English army marched into Scotland by land, under command of four assigned nobles, with men of lesser command and ten thousand troops, plus horsemen, to meet with the Reformers. By Saturday, tents appeared near Leith and cannons were readied for attack on the fortified town. The French, inside the fort, were preparing to hold out to the end with food supplies they had scavenged from the surrounding countryside before the final closing of gates.

Margaret felt an unshakable cloak of doom settling over her. She watched from the window, her eyes narrowing. At times, Lord Carlton would accompany her and study the manmade earthworks around Leith, along with the sea of tents sprawled in all directions. Somewhere in the maze, Lord Corleal could be settling in for battle.

With a growing attachment to Lord Carlton, Margaret studied the stooped shoulders, the black eyes now dulled by age. In nearly two years, she had developed a deep affection for him, for he had been kind to her, almost like a father. *I will miss him,* she thought, *when*—. She couldn't finish. She forced her dark thoughts elsewhere.

The old man reached over and patted her arm. "I don't know how I would pass my days without you," he said. "You have made my days brighter just by being here. Don't leave, Margaret," he pleaded. "Please don't leave us."

"I can't say how God will solve it," she answered softly, "but he will."

"Do you love that fellow, Corleal, that much, Margaret? Don't you have any love for my nephew, or am I badly mistaken when I see you look at him with your blue eyes—a look that speaks of more than friendship?"

"If Lord Ballender were my betrothed, and I were stolen away for two years, wouldn't you expect me to keep my promise?" she pursued softly.

"But you didn't say you loved your Englishman." He paused only slightly before probing, "Do you?"

"I—I was promised by my father at one week of age, my lord. Love was not a condition of the betrothal agreement."

"So you're willing to take a chance at this. It's best to love a man first and let that love grow."

"You loved your wife?" Margaret asked quietly.

"Aye. With all my heart."

Returning below, Margaret saw Anson waiting in the hall. Immediately she brought refreshments. Her uneasiness increased, bringing into focus the memory of the moments prior to her capture on the Corleal Road so long ago—the premonition that preceded her capture and subsequently altered her life so drastically.

"How is the Regent?" asked Lord Carlton, studying Anson.

"She has dropsy and is dying. Her legs are swollen and soft as butter."

"Those at the castle will see that she remains safe from her enemies."

Anson exhaled a prolonged sigh. "Her enemies are legion, my

friend. She has but three faithful friends left. The rest have departed from her due to her wretched lies."

"Cowards, all of them!" stormed the old man. "How is the battle going?"

"The French wreak a great amount of havoc from the fortifications and the artillery in the kirk steeple."

Before Margaret could return to the kitchen below, William intercepted her. "A messenger is waiting at the door for you," he told her quietly.

Her heart froze within her. "Did he give you a message or tell you his name?"

"No, Miss. Do you want me to accompany you?"

"Yes," her voice was husky as she formed an answer. "Please." Margaret moved mechanically to the door and saw a man standing there in the livery of an English servant.

"Margaret Chilton?" he inquired immediately.

"Yes, I am she." Her breathing was becoming labored with the accelerated beating of her heart. She waited for the inevitable words that followed.

"Lord Corleal sent me with this message. Please read it while I wait."

Margaret put out her hand woodenly for the paper, trying to calm her fingers as they ripped open the seal of the letter. She attempted to hold the message steady enough for her to make out the contents.

> Margaret,
>
> I am in the field outside Edinburgh and wish to see you. Please come to my tent with the servant who delivers this message to you. I shall be waiting.
>
> John Corleal

Margaret read the letter and folded it carefully, the lump in her throat threatening to choke her of all breath.

"Let me get my cloak," she answered calmly. Then turning to William she requested that he do one last errand for her, her face chalk-white as she faced him. "Please tell Lord Carlton good-by for me, after I leave, and inform him that I am being taken to Lord Corleal who waits for me in the field."

"Let me send a servant with you," William begged. "Milord would not want it otherwise."

Margaret nodded mutely. As she wrapped her cloak around her and waited for William to return with one of the men, she felt the tears form in her eyes. This may be good-by forever, she reasoned. I haven't even time to write Gavin a note—but I know not what I would write. Margaret was certain that he knew how she felt about him, but she could not put it into words—not on paper. *It's better that I go and try to forget him as quickly as possible.*

For a moment, Margaret stood near the door and glanced in at Lord Carlton sitting by the fire with his hands on the knob of his cane. Increasingly, his mind seemed to be on days past, when the country was at peace and he lived with the wife he loved. Little did he know that at this very moment Margaret was slipping out of his life as silently as she had entered it nearly two years before.

Pulling open the door, Margaret looked back through her tears at William and put her hand out to him. "If God wills it, I shall return," she said in farewell.

Lord Corleal's servant sat straight and unsmiling on his horse as he and Margaret and the servant from the mansion picked their way around the sedgy pools dotting the fields far behind the battle line. Her heart sat as stone within her breast. How long had Corleal known she was here? Lord Corleal hadn't even come the length of the town to claim her.

Margaret and the servants approached the great array of tents, moving toward an especially large one with two soldiers guarding the door. Margaret's mouth was powder dry as the two soldiers parted the tent flaps for her and she walked inside. Before her eyes adjusted fully she heard a sharp command. Immediately the two soldiers scurried away.

"Margaret," Lord Corleal said, nodding.

"Milord." He had changed little in two years other than the thinning of his hair and the added weight of his body. His movements remained slow and deliberate. He eyed her from the top of her head to her toes that extended beneath the silk of her dress.

"If you have changed," he replied tightly, studying her, "it's not visible." Then moving two chairs close together he admonished, "Be seated." Margaret obeyed mechanically, staring into the eyes of a man to whom she had been formally betrothed to marry for her whole lifetime.

He seemed a total stranger to her rather than the man to whom she was committed. When she sat down next to him, most wretchedly ill at ease, she dared to look into his face. After all the endless months of waiting, she found it hard to believe that he was actually in Scotland and talking with her.

"How did you find me?" she inquired, breaking the unbearable silence.

"I got a letter—belatedly, for it had been lost and someone found it. I was convinced it wasn't your handwriting. One of your father's servants relayed the events of your capture, when I found him bound with ropes the next day. I sent my soldiers to find you, but your captors kept you well hidden."

"I lived in the hut of a tailor, at first, and then was put in Ballender Castle before being brought here."

Lord Corleal's brows rose suspiciously. "No women were present?" An alarming churlishness spread over his face with the asking.

"Not in the hut, but Robin was a good man and treated me with respect."

"Did he—touch you?" he demanded, eyeing her critically from where he stood.

"No, milord."

"And Lord Ballender?" he questioned briskly.

"No."

"I find that hard to believe," he retorted irritably, "for I met him and he doesn't appear the type to leave a beautiful girl alone. He seems anything but a gentleman or honorable." Lord Corleal stated his opinions with rising ire.

Margaret sighed but held her peace.

"So," he snarled, "he did try to soil you."

"No," Margaret insisted through clenched teeth. She found it hard to accept this underlying condemnation of her unblemished conduct for the past two years.

"Ballender is handsome, isn't he?"

Margaret's eyes shot up to study the man, aware that he baited her and watched her quick reaction to his question. "Yes," she admitted.

"He has a lover, I'm told. Is it you?" The voice was menacingly low and caustic as he lifted his eyes to study her, waiting for her response.

"No, I am not," Margaret denied, her chin rising perceptibly.

"You are terribly defensive. I wonder why," he sneered. Then Lord Corleal came to observe her intently at close quarters. "You love him," he accused. "Can you deny it?" His voice was purposely quiet so the soldiers by the flaps would not hear him.

Margaret focused her eyes on Lord Corleal's face as the earth shook with the tremor from a cannonball, shot from one of the huge machines in Leith. She had been faithful to the end, though her heart yearned to reach out to Gavin. Surely a merciful God would not condemn her to a life of misery with this man—a man who watched her, accused her unreasonably, and displayed not one drop of love or compassion. When her lips parted to give him her answer, Margaret determined to be truthful.

"Before God," she began, "I have kept my body undefiled. But my heart, in spite of my desire otherwise, belongs to Lord Ballender," she whispered hoarsely. For just a moment, Margaret witnessed the unleashed fury of his breathing and she thought he was going to strike her for that blatant admission on her part. But the blow didn't come. Instead, the corners of Lord Corleal's mouth curved up slightly and formed a touch of a smile. It was frightening—and puzzling. If he had simply brought his hand cracking over her face—completing the act and then swinging away—she could have taken it. But he didn't.

"So," he answered, too calmly. "You want me to sever our betrothal and send you back to him. Right?"

Margaret remained silent, watching him pivot about slowly and face her squarely with his calm announcement. "Today I will travel into Edinburgh and make arrangements for our marriage and then you shall become my wife as soon as a priest can perform the ceremony."

Margaret felt all color drain from her face. She thought she was going to faint at his feet.

"And then," he informed her softly, "I shall see that our barbaric Lord Ballender comes to a tragic end so we need not have his face coming between us in our wedded bliss."

Margaret looked into the face of the man for whom she had waited so patiently for two long years of anxiety and frustration that had finally turned to dread. "Lord Ballender's servant waits for me outside," she whispered. "I must permit him to return to the mansion."

"I shall see to it," he snapped with the suddenness of a whip. "From now on, until you are my wife, you shall take care to stay in my tent, hidden from view of the rabble outside, for there are few women here, other than the sluts that follow the soldiers. My men will guard you day and night at the peril of their lives," he warned.

The dismissal of the Ballender servant was unduly harsh. Margaret cringed at both the needless fury flung at the frightened man and the fate, worse than death, that now faced her as Lord Corleal's wife.

In the afternoon, when the fighting waned, Lord Corleal ordered his servant to stay with Margaret as he prepared to ride into Edinburgh with two of his soldiers.

"You dare leave your post in the midst of battle?" she accused. "The Scots depend on your help to rid them of these French locusts—"

"As far as I'm concerned," he retorted, interrupting her with a haughty curl of his lip, "the French are not the threat that the barbaric Scots portrayed to our queen."

"You don't understand the situation with these wretched French!" she cried out in defense. "You haven't seen the Scots burned for their beliefs and the cause of Christ!"

"And I have no desire to be slaughtered for their cause—just or unjust—nor change my usual schedule and forego a few hours of my accustomed pleasure at dice." He tightened his doublet around his expanding middle and adjusted his sword for departure. Then he gathered Margaret to his chest and placed his lips on hers. The nearness of the man repulsed her, but she dared not pull loose for fear he would do worse. Margaret remained in his arms, stiff and barely yielding.

When he flung her from him, she leaned against the wooden tent pole and placed her hands over her mouth to still the quivering— the anguish that filled her soul. *O God, how can I endure this?*

The afternoon was cold with a mist of rain coating the tent, as well as the soldiers standing sentry. Perhaps she could bribe them to let her escape. Logic told her, however, that they would pay with their lives for such a breach of conduct. She couldn't jeopardize their lives for her own personal desires. And Samuel . . . but that was pure folly; he was blindly loyal to his master.

When the rain eased and the old servant picked up a pail to fetch water for the evening meal, Margaret fell back on the one wide mat and closed her eyes to think. Was there no means of escaping this prison?

She helped Samuel prepare the evening meal over his adamant objections to the idea that Lord Corleal's betrothed would cook. His shock provided a slight touch of levity in an otherwise unamusing situation.

Samuel was spooning a stew onto metal plates when a thunderous stamping of hoofs reached their ears, accompanied by musket fire and voices shouting, "Siege!" In the absence of their commanding officer, the Corleal troops had lapsed into a general laxness, but now they raced to snatch up their weapons and fire blindly at the fleeing enemy.

Rushing to the tent door, Margaret and Samuel observed a

general slaughter as a result of the surprise attack by the invading French horsemen—a massacre that left dozens dead and wounded before the enemy fled back to the protective wall of the fort.

"Milord!" screamed Samuel, recognizing the body of his master. Two soldiers carefully placed Corleal on his cot as Margaret and Samuel rushed to unfasten his blood-soaked doublet.

chapter
26

LORD CORLEAL REGAINED full consciousness three days later as the English bombardment of Leith toppled the artillery-filled steeple of the kirk. "As soon as I can be up," he stated flatly, "we will be married and then return to my castle. This war is nearly over."

"I pray it is true, but how can you be so certain?"

"Our ships are blockading the Firth beyond Leith, and the French can no longer receive fresh supplies of men, artillery, or food."

"They have driven enough cattle into the city—cattle they stole from the poor farmers for miles around Edinburgh—to last for some time," objected Margaret.

"For a town the size of Leith, supplies can't last long. No, they will soon surrender."

The end of this horrible war will be a blessing to everyone but me. She had no desire to return to Corleal Castle as Lady Corleal. Not once had the man told her he loved her—nor even passed her a tender or kind look. He wanted to marry her only to punish her—to keep her from going to Lord Ballender.

The war continued; Lord Corleal made slow progress toward recovery; the siege of Leith dragged on—but Margaret's thoughts were forever on Gavin and his uncle. If only she could be allowed one parting good-by—one tender kiss from Gavin to sustain her for the loveless years that faced her as Lord Corleal's wife. With the warmth of the sun on her face, Margaret closed her eyes against the brightness of its rays and asked God to deliver her.

"The city is afire!" someone shouted, causing Margaret's eyes to snap open. "Look!" The sky was painted orange from flames shooting up above the battlements of the city, feeding on powdery-dry timbers and thatched roofs that were ready tinder.

But the citizens' suffering was not yet at an end. The week following the fire, the Scottish and English troops readied for a combined assault on Leith.

Lord Corleal walked outside his tent to observe preparations and to try riding, as a test of his ability to make the long trip back to Corleal. The soldiers turned hostile eyes upon their commander. An undercurrent of hatred due to the large number of deaths and disabling wounds as a result of his negligence in duty during the surprise attack had begun to infiltrate the troops.

Margaret's betrothed ordered his aged servant to go into Edinburgh to arrange for a priest to marry her and Lord Corleal the next day in the kirk. When he returned he reported the arrangements were complete, and in his arms, he carried a lovely gown of green velvet trimmed in pearls.

"This," Lord Corleal informed Margaret, "is your wedding dress." If only Gavin were presenting the magnificent gown, she would have been delighted. But she found no pleasure in receiving it from a man with no affection for her. She forced herself to say, "Thank you, milord."

Corleal's eyes smoldered with anger, but he kept his voice low. "You show cool gratitude for a penniless bride." Then he smiled. "But you will earn the right to wear this garment. I am a man of insatiable appetites, as you will discover."

Margaret thought her heart would burst with the anguish building up inside her.

"You can play the jealous wife," he added dryly, "but you will learn to adjust. You have your Ballender; I have another as well."

"Then why, milord," Margaret asked pleadingly, daring to reason with him concerning her fate, "don't you give me to the man I love?"

"Because not every man can be so fortunate as to have a beautiful wife gracing his castle. And so virtuous—if I can believe what you tell me." With this, he reached over and lifted her chin so their eyes met. An evil smile turned his lips up at the corners to challenge her avowal. "I will know soon enough, won't I?"

A deep shudder ran the full length of her body. She heard his laughter long after he fell asleep on his mat and she lay on hers. Margaret wondered what the old servant, on his mat by the door, thought when he heard the lord mock her. At times Samuel treated her kindly, especially when Lord Corleal slept or was not aware of what his servant was doing. Could the old man be counted on to help her if she desperately needed it?

The combined Scottish and English troops had dug trenches deep into the earth near the walls of Leith. Cannons were moved into position for battering the high southwest wall. Scaling ladders lay constructed and awaiting the moment the men would attempt to divert the French along the northwest seawall by climbing over the battlements at low tide. At this point, the attackers tensely awaited the signal to begin.

Lord Corleal rose and dressed for his wedding, instructing Margaret to do the same. Since he could not return to battle, he ordered his possessions packed before daybreak and moved well enough behind the lines so he could start, without delay, for Corleal Castle immediately after the ceremony.

"There is nothing to be afraid of," Lord Corleal assured his betrothed, his lips pressed in a firm line. He urged Margaret to accompany him for one final, closer look at the battle preparations among the earthworks on the road leading to Leith.

"The signal to bombard will not be given yet. By the time it's given, we will be in Edinburgh," he told her, chiding her for her childish fears. "The day's slaughter will end this ridiculous war and our soldiers will be able to go back home where they belong."

But as they approached the trenches, the cannons on the battlements of Leith suddenly burst the air with their thunderous roars. Volleys were returned. Instantly the battle raged savagely all around as Corleal sought to escape. The fear etched on his face was the last thing Margaret remembered before the ugly scene was completely blasted from her memory.

Margaret was vaguely aware of gentle hands applying damp cloths to her face, but she was unable to respond to those around her. At times warm liquid trickled down her throat and pale lights shone from somewhere in the gossamer haze of puzzling confusion. She tried to sit up, but the onrushing pain and nausea overwhelmed her and she fell back instantly.

"Lie still, Margaret," said a familiar voice by the bed. She turned suddenly to see Lord Carlton beside her.

"Is it really you?" she asked weakly, hardly daring to believe she was actually back in Edinburgh.

"Aye, and I'm greatly relieved to see you with us again. Is the pain great?" His words were kind and gentle.

"How did the battle go?" Margaret asked, recalling the last few moments before she was hit.

"Not well, my dear. Not well. The many confusing signals among the troops led to heavy losses to both English and Scots. Apparently the Englishmen who were to scale the sea walls didn't do what was commanded. The noblemen claimed the ladders were too short. I don't know. Our soldiers said the women of Leith threw stones on them, then tossed fire and timber at our own men.

"That slut, Betty Stanus, was one of those screaming obscenities. I knew she was no good," he added with a scowl. "Now the whole world knows it. And when the battle ended," he said bitterly, a tear trickling from his eye, "our despicable Regent, watching from the castle, screamed for joy when she saw the number of dead. The French were so boastful the next day, that they even went out to pick up cockles on the shore." He sighed heavily. "What a blind old fool I've been."

"How did I get here?" Margaret asked suddenly.

"Your Corleal was killed, Margaret, and a weeping old man came to ask if he could bring you here to me.

"And—Lord Ballender?" she hardly dared breathe. "Is he well?"

"I pray so, my dear. I've not seen him," the old man answered sadly. "When he learned that you were gone, he left and hasn't been back."

"We—we did not marry, Lord Corleal and I. There was no longer any affection between the two of us," Margaret explained, her voice weak, yet filled with relief.

"Aye. That is understandable. You never should have left us, Margaret. Your place is here." Then, rising, he said, "You must rest now so you get well."

She closed her eyes and wished desperately that Gavin would come, for she must know how he felt toward her. If he no longer wanted her, she would have nowhere to go. *O Lord, I am at your mercy. Please help me,* she pleaded as she drifted back into sleep once more.

The winds of July shifted, bringing rain. Margaret lit a fire in the hall grate to rid the room of its chill before she sat down to read to Lord Carlton. She noticed that he no longer shouted at William or the servants since he started attending preaching at St. Giles. His smile of contentment now permeated the mansion and sent a wave of calm where previously there was unbearable tension. When Margaret saw his head begin to nod, she placed the book on the table near the old man's chair and moved silently from the room, up the winding stairs, to her room.

She barely pulled the covers over her arms before slipping into a deep sleep. How long she slumbered, she didn't know, but suddenly she saw someone in the darkened room beside her bed. Could she be dreaming? Then the familiarity of the shape pierced her senses and she cried out, "Gavin? Is—is it you?" A bowman could feel no more tension in the taut bowstring at his fingertips than she felt at the sight of the muscular form silhouetted against the light. With her hand, Margaret pushed back the covering and rose slowly, unsteadily, to her feet. She waited for him to speak.

"You know the French have surrendered?" he said quietly.

"Yes, I was told," she answered. *Why was he so maddeningly calm?* Her eyes studied him as he walked to the window and stared out. She had thought of no one but him for months past and her life had been miserable because of it. Now he had suddenly reappeared into her life and spoken to her as he would a mere acquaintance. *Does he no longer feel any love for me? Is that what he is preparing to tell me?* A sickening feeling threatened to engulf her whole being.

Without warning he turned about and walked toward her, to stand so near her bed that she could easily reach out her hand and touch him. "Did you also know that the Regent is dead and the French have left our country?"

"Yes," Margaret whispered with a sinking heart, expecting the next words to be a total, swift rejection of her. She swallowed and tried to rid her throat of the powdery dryness choking her.

"Margaret," he pleaded suddenly, "Why did you leave me?"

"Lord Corleal sent his servant to bring me to him," she explained softly, her voice straining.

"Did you marry Corleal?" Gavin demanded.

"No." Margaret shook her head as she answered. "He questioned me and asked if I—" She bit her lip and let her lashes sweep her cheeks.

"If you what?" Gavin's eyes didn't once move from her face.

"If I loved you," she whispered.

"And—"

"I answered—that I did." Margaret's eyes assessed his face as she spoke the words that told of the state of her heart. She watched the hint of a grin curl up the corners of his mouth until a triumphant smile reached his eyes.

In the next instant she was aware that his arms reached out for her. He pulled her roughly toward him and clasped her tightly to his chest. "Oh, my love," Gavin breathed hoarsely.

Margaret was aware that he felt the willingness of her lips meeting his as his face lowered eagerly toward hers. Then, still holding her closely, she heard him tell of the anguish that had overtaken him when he'd learned that she had left his uncle's house and gone to Corleal.

"I would have completely lost my reason," Gavin admitted painfully, his face brushing against the softness of her hair. "In my hopelessness I appealed to God for help, for I knew you loved me. Of that I was certain beyond a doubt. So, to trust God was my total consolation."

Holding her at arm's length, he searched her face a moment before continuing. Then cupping her face with his hands, he gently lifted her head in order to gaze into the depths of her eyes. "Will you be my wife, Margaret?"

She looked up into the handsome face of the man she had loved for so long, her eyes sparkling with tears of deep happiness. "Yes—oh, yes," she cried. "How long I've wanted to tell you that!"

ABOUT THE AUTHOR

JEANNE CHEYNEY is a former teacher and librarian who now spends much of her time writing and illustrating educational books with her husband. In addition to writing, she enjoys raising quail, making puppets, and painting with watercolors.

Cheyney and her husband backpacked through Scotland, following the routes of the Reformers and of the border reivers, before she wrote *Captive's Promise*. This is her second Serenade Saga; the first was *The Conviction of Charlotte Grey*.

A Letter to Our Readers

Dear Reader:

Welcome to Serenade Books—a series designed to bring you beautiful love stories in the world of inspirational romance. They will uplift you, encourage you, and provide hours of wholesome entertainment, as thousands of readers have testified. That we might better contribute to your reading enjoyment, we would appreciate your taking a few minutes to respond to the following questions and return to:

> Lois Taylor
> Serenade Books
> Zondervan Publishing House
> 1415 Lake Drive, S.E.
> Grand Rapids, Michigan 49506

1. Did you enjoy reading *Captive's Promise?*

   ☐ Very much. I would like to see more books by this author!
   ☐ Moderately
   ☐ I would have enjoyed it more if _____

2. Where did you purchase this book? _____

3. What influenced your decision to purchase this book?

   ☐ Cover   ☐ Back cover copy
   ☐ Title   ☐ Friends
   ☐ Publicity   ☐ Other _____

4. Please rate the following elements from 1 (poor) to 10 (superior).

- ☐ Heroine   ☐ Plot
- ☐ Hero   ☐ Inspirational theme
- ☐ Setting   ☐ Secondary characters

5. What are some inspirational themes you would like to see treated in future books?

_____

_____

6. Please indicate your age range:

- ☐ Under 18   ☐ 25–34   ☐ 46–55
- ☐ 18–24   ☐ 35–45   ☐ Over 55

Serenade / Saga books are inspirational romances in historical settings, designed to bring you a joyful, heart-lifting reading experience.

Serenade / Saga books available in your local bookstore:

Serenade/Saga books are now being published in a new, longer length:

Serenade / Serenata books are inspirational romances in contemporary settings, designed to bring you a joyful, heart-lifting reading experience.

Serenade / Serenata books available in your local bookstore:

#29 *Born to Be One,* Cathie LeNoir
#30 *Heart Aflame,* Susan Kirby
#31 *By Love Restored,* Nancy Johanson
#32 *Karaleen,* Mary Carpenter Reid
#33 *Love's Full Circle,* Lurlene McDaniel
#34 *A New Love,* Mab Graff Hoover
#35 *The Lessons of Love,* Susan Phillips
#36 *For Always,* Molly Noble Bull
#37 *A Song in the Night,* Sara Mitchell
#38 *Love Unmerited,* Donna Fletcher Crow
#

#

...ed in a new,

lo

Date Due

5/29			
SEP 18 1988			
NOV 13 1988			
1-29-80			
JUN 17 1990			
FEB 2 3 1992			

BRODART, INC.   Cat. No. 23 233   Printed in U.S.A.